PEMAQUID

Their Light Of Love

By

R.W. Secor

1

Marilyn pulled into the gravel parking lot like she owned the place. Yet this was her first visit to Pemaquid Lighthouse. She had spent years researching Maine lighthouses, but never spent a minute in Maine. Growing up on the west coast of the US, lighthouses were not an uncommon sight. That is at least for those without their head down in their phone or their mind engrossed in social media. While it seemed impossible to drive by a forty-foot masterpiece without noticing it many did every day. Her father was a lighthouse inspector. He was a lens specialist, only one of a handful in the US with the qualifications to inspect all types of lighthouses, as well as repair and renew from the footer to tip of the cupola.

As a young girl she was "forced" to travel with her father. However, to her there was no force involved. A single parent since Marilyn was five, her father had been gone often prior to the accident. After the accident he vowed never to be away from his family again. So, Marilyn became his road partner as they journeyed up and down the west coast. He was also her teacher and best friend. Maybe only friend, other than her lighthouses. She often remembered the first time she had looked up, standing at the base of Anacapa Lighthouse. It may sound strange but she felt as if she were looking up at her mom again. Seeing the structure, tall and strong, a warmth came over her, she felt safe and secure as she walked in and climbed slowly to the top with her father. As he worked on the light, she looked out over Arch Rock and the Santa Barbara Channel. Just like her mother used to protect her, the lighthouse protected all those who sailed in the area. She, the lighthouse, saved thousands of lives just like her mother saved Marilyn when their car was hit and veered into the canal full of water. Everyone told her it was a miracle her mother was able to get her out of the car and to the bank before she fell asleep and went to heaven. Although every lighthouse may be different they all save lives, and for Marilyn that embodied her mom.

After Marilyn received a degree in engineering, just like her father did decades earlier, she never entertained any other career choice. As a result she started researching lighthouses around the world. That is how she found those of Maine and especially Pemaquid. If only she could be for the east coast what her father was for the west. When she got the call to work on the Maine lighthouses, she was ecstatic until she realized she would have to say goodbye to her father and travel across the country. Fortunately he gave her his blessing and was as proud as any father could be. They had given their lives to each other for 20 years but they both knew it was time for her to follow her dreams.

2

Greg grew up in Bristol, Maine, the son of a lobster fisherman. After the age of 15 he spent more time on the water than land most days. He knew everything about Maine lobsters and the business. His college was the waters of the North Atlantic Ocean. While most college kids think their class load will kill them, for Greg his college actually claimed the lives of many over the years. He himself had had close calls, some so close he thought he was going to join those who never return to port. He too had a special affection for Pemaquid for it was her light that led him home many times over the years. So, when she needed a new keeper he volunteered even before he knew it was a paid job, with benefits. Something he had never thought about. He had looked at life as something one either lives or dies at. All in every day.

Maine produces over approximately ninety percent of US lobsters. It is a billion-dollar industry for the state shipping lobsters around the world. Maine claims to have the sweetest, best tasting lobster in the world. Strict harvesting laws had strengthened the fishery to a point better than ever in recorded history. This had made Greg and his fellow fisherman wealthy along the way. At least for the time being. One bad year could change everything for most of them, and they knew it. Bad years had ruined many others in the past. However for Greg, he had duties other than just lobstering.

Today was dusting day. The small educational and

informational room open to the public seemed to gather dust by the second.   As a result every few days it needed and deserved a good dusting. Can in one hand and rag in other Greg went to town gathering as much dust as he could. Polishing everything to a shine, his results would be envied by the best of shoe shiners everywhere. Also he repositioned things left askew by visitors that just could not follow the signs of No Touching. Actually, he did not blame them, some things just needed to be touched to fully appreciate. Besides, the more visitors that came, and returned, the more he could substantiate the need to keep the lighthouse open for the public to the local historical society. Funds were getting harder to come by due to everyone wanting a piece of the pie. Every year something else was being nominated for historical status. This was common along the east coast. In fact giving up his salary had crossed his mind if needed to save Pemaquid.

3

"Welcome to Pemaquid Point Light. Have you been here in the past?" Greg asked.

"No, my first time. It's marvelous. Just as I remembered it." Marilyn responded.

This started a back and forth quick banter.

"I thought you said you've never been here before."

"That's right. I take it from the dust rag you work here?"

"You could say that. Anything you would like to know?"

"No. I know all about her."

"Never been here but know all about her. Take it you're from the city."

"You could say that."

"Well, if you have any questions…"

She turned before he finished and went outside to walk around the grounds and get a view from all angles. She could tell from the ground the type of lens, but she also knew from her studies of the lighthouse. The sun was shining off the glass and she could feel the warmth on her shoulders. The sound of waves crashing against the rocks was dancing in her head. The lighthouse was far better than she had imagined from the pictures.

4

The lighthouse light is what makes the lighthouse. While that may sound obvious, the type of light has varied over the past 300 plus years. Actually lighthouses date back thousands of years. The house part was not used as much early on. The light often was just wood burning on a shore line, there to mark dangerous waters and/or navigational routes and harbors. Over time the lights were used more often and relied on by sailors. As with any growing need, the service became more important and in turn more resources were spent on the lights.

The lights needed protection from the elements of nature and were expected to be working at all times. Thus, they became enclosed and eventually surrounded by glass. Light keepers were put in place for 24-hour care of the light. Improving visualization of the light by the sailors was a continual challenge to those who designed the light. Although, many ways of getting the light higher in altitude and brighter were tried, the lighthouse structure won out eventually for most. However, there are definitely regional preferences for how the lighthouse should be built around the world. An enclosed, continuous high light was not the end of the design concern. Next was a need for the light to be seen even further out to sea.

Wood was the primary fuel for hundreds, probably thousands, of years. Eventually other products were tried and found both easier to use and to provide a brighter light. Coal, tallow and wax candles, animal and vegetable oils, kerosene, acetylene and eventually electricity were all used. Sperm whale oil, from the head of the whale, was the mainstay for many decades. Using one or multiple wicks, whale oil was dependable, cleaner burning and easier to set up a continuous self-supply of oil after filling a reservoir. Next came the lens, to both collect the light and make it shine even further into the night.

As electricity became more available around the world, it was only time before it took over lighthouses. Many different electric lamps were tried and used but still it was the lens that really made the difference. In its ability to collect and focus the light into a lifesaving beam. The lens that won over all the others was the Fresnel lens. It has been modified over the years but still remains the gold standard in lighthouse lenses. There are many different sizes and types based on the original bullseye design. Each has provided life saving improvements.

5

Marilyn checked into the Pemaquid Hotel, just a 2-minute walk from the lighthouse on Pemaquid Point. Pemaquid is the Abenaki Indian word meaning "situated far out". She would use this as her base for her stay in Maine for now. She was only a few miles from the Village of New Harbor for any other needs. Traveling with her father had taught her to pack light. She definitely was not a valley girl with bag after bag packed full for even a short travel. Since she had a small kitchen in her room, she would get some essentials in town, and then check in with the Lighthouse Commission, controlled by the United States Coast Guard(USCG). It was the Maine Lights Program that led the way in the US, and provided an example for other countries, in the preservation of lighthouses. The job Marilyn was facing would be demanding. There are five thousand miles of Maine coast line, with all the inlets and points, and over 60 lighthouses to monitor.

The USCG controls all lights of the US. Not all are functional, nor will they be again. But for those that are, they must be maintained. To do this, it is easier to hire outside experts. Local non-profit organizations also work with the USCG to keep lighthouses up and running, give tours when able and safe, raise money to help keep up the lighthouse and grounds. At times there can be differences of opinion, to say the least, as to who has the most vested interest in the lighthouse and should be in control. But unless the USCG sells the lighthouse, they remain in control. Since Marilyn was contracted by the USCG, she would be in charge of all maintenance to both the lighthouse and grounds.

The stop at the commission office was just like on the west coast only this time she was signing the paperwork instead of her father. She got the list of which lighthouses they wanted her to see first, then she was to review the rest in any order she desired. Some would take a day, others about a week. Her contract with the USCG was for a year with a floating end date, dependent on what she found. The hope was when done with Maine she would go on down the coast if she and the coast guard were happy with what was being done. Eventually she would like to have the contract for the entire east coast. By then she would hire a staff to help with routine lighthouses, thus giving her more time with problem lights and the most difficult part of the job, politics. Who would be best to partner with for care of the lighthouse; and even which to sell and to whom? Though she hated to see them sold, the new buyer would usually hire her father to continue maintenance, and she hoped the same would be the case for her. Unless the owner was a private buyer who did not want to keep the light active. Some were even demolished for the land. Although legal, it is very sad every time a lighthouse is lost.

6

"OK. Quiet down please. We are going to start the meeting." announced Fred, the president of the Pemaquid Light Society. This was a group of locals who volunteered to help keep the Pemaquid lighthouse running. They had no official regulatory abilities, but felt that if they did a good job for free, they would have some say in the future of the lighthouse. Besides who knows best other than the locals. So far, their plan was working.

Fred continued, "Now with roll call and the reading of the minutes over let's get down to new business. As most of you have heard, the commission is facing financial budgeting constraints again. A limited amount of money can only be spread so far effectively. So, we need more money from the federal government through the Unites States Coast Guard, or more local funds allocated to us from the local government, or we need to come up with the funds ourselves. Seems to be more groups after federal and local funding. And now with politicians promising reparations for votes, we do not know where the money will ultimately go after each election."

Sally spoke up, "I thought we were protected by the parks department to have sufficient funding."

Fred agreed but added, "The catch there is what is sufficient funding, and lights do not have tenure, so to speak, they can be decommissioned and closed or sold if their attendance or use does not substantiate continuing the program in the eyes of someone higher in the decision making process."

Another member asked, "Could we just buy the lighthouse and run it ourselves?"

Fred answered, "In theory that is possible. The Maine Lighthouse Program was established by Congress in 1996 after many years of fighting to save Maine lighthouses. It led to the National Historic Lighthouse Preservation Act (NHLPA) in 2000, to help save all US lights. When a light is considered not needed but can be designated historical, then a group may apply to become the guardian of the grounds. But there are no set rules, it becomes a decision by someone or a group in government to allow guardianship. If not, then the grounds may be sold. When lighthouses are put up for sale, they usually give preference to preservation groups, but do not have to. That is when politics, shall we say, enters the picture. We all know the value of any coastal property is more than we could every buy on our own. We would have a tough time with upkeep costs alone, even if given the property. Not to mention care keeper salary."

With that, many eyes looked in Greg's direction, while some put their heads down not wanting to confront him and the possibility of letting him go. As with most groups, especially non-profit, only a handful of individuals spend the time needed to keep the mission going. Hoping many will pitch in when needed. Few knew just how much day to day work was needed to keep a lighthouse operational. If most were willing to turn the light off, just to keep the building, in the past that was the end of larger donors and government support. So, it is either do it right or not at all.

Greg spoke up, "You all know I am willing to give up the job if needed to save the lighthouse."

Fred, "Nonsense. We need a keeper. Without one the gradual disrepair will accumulate to the point of condemnation. Good intentions only go so far. I can name other lighthouses lost due to this way of thinking. Not to disregard any of you or our other volunteers. We need to find a way to make this lighthouse valuable to most everyone, not just a few."

With that came silence. They all knew he was correct, but none knew how to solve the problem. They agreed more thought was needed for a new approach to save the lighthouse. The meeting ended with more apprehension than hope from the members.

7

Marilyn decided to drive north along the coast, to the US Canada border, to see West Quoddy Head Lighthouse; and see the lay of the coastline and experience the drive north. Most lights are north of Pemaquid, so she knew she would be driving this route often. Paradoxical to its name the West Quoddy Head Light is actually the easternmost beacon in the US. It also is one of the first to have installed a fog bell, since the area is covered with heavy fog so often. Early in its use, sailors would fire off a weapon to signal the keeper to start ringing the bell. Over the years fog signals became automated along with the lights. Though Marilyn's specialty was the light, fog signals fell under her knowledge and care as well.

Today the sun was shining bright, no fog in sight. The rare colored red and white striped light house with black gallery walk around the base of the lensed lamp area and red cupola on top was visible for miles without the light today. As Marilyn sat in the grass looking up at the lighthouse something different happened. Normally nothing could interrupt her admiration of such a monument. But today, as a single beam of light cut through a sliver of clouds so did a thought. No matter how hard she tried to suppress it, it would continue to return. She could not help thinking of Greg.

Marilyn had dated but not seriously. She was always on the move with her father, then off to college where she studied hard taking full loads. She knew the cost was significant for her father. She would not waste time on frivolous activities. Plus, she worked odd jobs along the way.   After college she interned with her father then obtained this job. She was sure his name influenced her hiring and she was not going to let him down. She had a job to do and no time for anything else right now. But…she wondered how he was doing.

8

Lobster fishing in Maine is generational into the 5th or more these days. Greg does it because it's what his family has done. He never had any thought, desire or yearning to do anything else. Only a person growing up in a generational business truly understands this feeling. He is happiest on the water, and especially when bringing up pots, the traps used to catch the lobsters.

The pots have a bag of cut fish for bait usually. They sit on the bottom, the lobsters crawl in looking for the bait. Small ones are able to get out small holes to get away from the bigger lobsters. Lobsters will eat each other if need be. The pots are put out as singles with a rope up to the surface attached to a float called a buoy; or on a long line with an anchor on one end and a buoy on the other with multiple traps a set distance along the line. Either way, one starts by hooking the line at the buoy then placing the line over a pulley and then the line runs through a motorized winch. The buoy can be thrown back in the water if resetting the trap after removing caught lobsters. So, one can empty, check the bait and just push the trap back into the water. The buoys are marked by color or tags as to whom they belong to. That way everyone knows whose traps are whose, especially after a big storm when they may have been moved about. All of this was usually done with a driver and at least one deck hand.

The lobsters all must be measured for legal size to keep. The back of the shell, carapace, must be three and a quarter to five inches in length, too small or large then back into the water. A female with eggs has a v notch cut on her tail and is released, so when caught next time and if does not have eggs she will still be released since she is a known breeding female. This helps with sustainability and keeps all the lobstermen, of either gender, in business for future generations. Other areas of the US, or countries, may have different regulations and methodologies.

Greg was working by himself today, taking his time, and enjoying the catch. It was a good one today. As he drove from one area of pots to the next, he gazed into the shoreline shining in the sun, happy he did not have to work on land. Even when it was cold, raining, extremely hot, there were high waves or anything that made pulling pots harder, he still would take this over that. As he pulled in his last trap, he got a surprise. A blue lobster. Some say it is a one in a million catch. But he had known others that had caught one. It was his first. Others say they taste better but he would not find out. Old fisherman's lore says there is good luck on the way for the lobsterman who catches a blue. As he looked at the brilliant blue in the afternoon sun, he could only see it going into the Pemaquid Museum tank for now. Hopefully it would bring good luck for the entire park, as well as an educational draw for more visitors.

9

Greg could hear someone downstairs. The museum
was not open yet so no one should be down there. Is it
a burglar? Nautical items, especially old ones, have
great value on the open and black market. Greg crept
down the stairs ever so slowly and quietly. He held a
fish club in his hand ready to use it if needed. As he
peeked around the corner at the bottom of the stairs, he
recognized her, even from behind. He could not resist.
He jumped out of the dark into the dim light with club
raised and a shrieking cry that would make every brave
Apache warrior proud, at least in any western he had
seen. She jumped, gave out her own shriek, and
promptly hit Greg on the head with the item in her hand.
A cast iron six-pound cannon ball, small for cannon
balls but more than enough to put Greg on his knees, or
his Prayer handles as the locals call them.

He moaned, "What the hell was that? Damn I think
I'm bleeding?"

Marilyn responded, "Oops!"

"Oops? That is all you have to say after cracking
my head wide open?" he demanded.

By now she had the light on her phone beaming in
his eyes and then to the wound. "You mean this little
scratch? I barley hit you!"

Another round of banter.

"Then why are my eyes watering and I have blood
on my fingers?"

"Because you rather juvenilishly tried to scare me. And I do not like being scared."

"You don't seem too concerned about almost killing me."

"If I wanted to kill you, I would not have stopped after the first hit!"

"Whatever. Why did you break in and try to steal whatever you hit me with?"

"First, I did not break in, the door was unlocked. And second, I did not steal anything."

"Because I stopped you."

"You stopped me! I'm not the one on the floor!"

"OK. Maybe I forgot to lock up last night. I need to get up." Greg used the fish club as a cane to help pushing himself up onto his feet.

"Were you actually going to hit me with that fish kill club?"

"No! But sorta wish I did now."

"Sort of."

"That's what I said, sorta."

Marilyn shook her head. Who taught these people how to talk? She helped Greg to a chair and examined his near mortal wound again. And again, it was just a superficial scratch at best. The blood was already gone. She checked his eyes, pupils equal and responded briskly. Her college first aid class, that she at the time felt it was a waste of her time, actually helped her with what to do next. Which was a series of questions checking memory and judgment. Ending with, "And are you going to try this stunt again someday?"

"Not with you! You're no fun."

"You do not even know me. How would you know how fun I am?"

"Hitting people with…" He was looking around. "A Civil War cannon ball is not fun!"

"Actually, at the time of your attack I was thinking, this seemed a bit small to be a cannon ball, but I guess it was not after all. It was enough to disable you."

Greg moaned, "Why are you here?"

"Yes. Almost forgot. I need your help."

"You have a strange way of asking someone for help."

"Well you started it with all that screaming and the club. Scaring people is not your strong suit."

"How would you know what my strong suit is?"

"I asked around. I am not going to just ask a stranger, key word strange," she said with a laugh, "for help with my work."

"What work would that be."

"I am the lighthouse inspector hired by the state to inspect all Maine lighthouses."

"What happened to Guy, key word guy."

"So, you don't think a woman can do the job?"

"The last guy's name was Guy! And he never hit me with anything." he smirked.

"Are you going to keep harping on that? It was nothing. He, Guy, retired is what I was told."

"I take it you need a chauffeur to get to the island lights?"

"See, that brain of yours is working just fine. When can we get started?" she said.

"How about tomorrow morning about 8? Tide should be best then."

"It's a date. Well, you know what I mean." She said hesitantly.

"Date it is. Do you know where my boat is in the marina?"

"I told you I did my homework. Meet you there at eight, and it's not a real date. It's work."

"Then you won't mind helping check my pots, since it's work."

"Whatever you want."

10

Greg laid in bed thinking about Maine's lighthouses. How could Maine be Maine without lighthouses. He knew Maine was much more than just the lights. And the lights were antiquated compared to modern GPS(Global Positioning System). Anyone with a cell phone could know exactly where they were in the world, as long as they had a signal. Truly amazing. But back to what all Maine had to offer.

He tried to think of all he knew Maine was well known for, as well as not so well known for. The lobster industry was probably number one. Especially for him since that is how he made a living. It was his world so to say. But he had been reminded by farmers that though Maine supplied ninety percent of the US lobsters, they supplied ninety nine percent of the US blueberries, as well as a top producer of potatoes and broccoli. And the foresters supplied ninety percent of the US toothpicks. So, maybe they all were close enough to call it a tie. Besides, what's best after a lobster meal, with potatoes and broccoli of course? A piece of blueberry pie, and then a toothpick to finish off the meal. The hikers knew Maine for the end of the Appalachian Trail, at Mount Katahdin. All outdoors people had heard of the great footwear and clothing made in Maine. Then there were over three thousand islands. Most visitors were unaware of that fact. The islands made navigating the shoreline troublesome most of the time, but they too were good landmarks. Both are reasons why so many lighthouses are on an island.

All of this was great but the problem remained how to make the lighthouses relevant and valuable to the everyday person in Maine, local or visitor. As with most issues it comes down to money. There is no mission without money. In this case, it is the lack of money that literally makes the lighthouses go away. If there were a way to make the lighthouses needed by the people of the state then the government would foot the cost of upkeep. If there were a way to make the lighthouses wanted by the people then they would foot the cost. And if both could be achieved that would best assure the continuation of the lighthouses in Maine.

He mused, what about weather and/or traffic stations. Maybe use the lights as the reference points along the coast for where the weather changes, and where traffic patterns change. If the news would use them as reference points daily on broadcasts, everyone would come to depend on them and their locations. Or maybe replace the light windows with solar panels to provide electricity for the light and grounds, maybe even put electricity back into the grid to help with electric costs for those in the area. Greg thought he better start writing these ideas down so he would not forget. He reached for his phone to dictate his thoughts without having to actually write them down on paper. Again, Greg realized smart phones are amazing. There's another idea! Use a phone app to integrate all the things people could use the lights for to make their lives easier and more fun. It is going to be a long night, he thought.

11

Marilyn and Greg were not the only ones meeting that morning. The Governor had called in her committee of budgetary advisers to discuss state budget issues, in Augusta, the capital of Maine. Budgetary cuts was the topic of the day. Governor Jane Capp tapped the almost two hundred year old gavel on the worn wooden table of the same era. She called the meeting to order and began her well thought out and rehearsed speech to the members of the committee. Though she was a born and raised Mainer, only half her ancestry was actually from Maine, the other hailed from NY City. She campaigned using every bit of the first half, but lived by the latter half. Her primary ambitions and goals had been accomplished throughout her long career. She had just one more, to move to 1600 Pennsylvania Avenue. And she would do so by any means necessary. Including letting every lighthouse in Maine crumble in disrepair if she felt the money allocated for them would better suit her ambitions elsewhere.

"Any questions?" Capp asked.

"Yes." a member quickly asked, "What about our lighthouses? You failed to mention anything about any of our programs to save the lights."

Capp responded someone indignantly, "That's actually the answer. Multiple programs and no results. The lack of community support indicates the lights are no longer a concern of the public, thus should not be a concern of ours. The cost of upkeep far out-paces that of income from the lights. It's time to put that money to better use for our citizens."

Another member spoke up, "You can not do that. The Maine Lights program was tenured years ago. We must set a budget for the program."

"I have looked into that. It was an unofficial designation. I am sure with good intentions, but there was never a vote recorded or registered. It is time to move into this century. With GPS the lights serve no use. They are expensive eye candy at best, much too expensive. They can be replaced by structures with much more use for our communities." Capp assured.

"Why can't the volunteer groups take over all the lights? They have done a good job with the ones they care for now." Another member asked.

"Actually they have not. Most are in need of structural repair. They do not have the funds to repair them. I know this because they have asked us to help. The liability of injury on the grounds is just too much for us to keep them open. Unless they can find a way to make the lighthouse more valuable than the land they sit on." She paused awkwardly, she did not mean to say what she was actually thinking. "I mean to pay for all upkeep to meet standards for a public building, that is what they need to fulfill to continue running the programs. If not the lands will be taken over by the state to protect the people from injury."

The room was silent for a few seconds that felt like minutes to everyone in the meeting. This was not the first time Capp had brought up the value of the land the lights were located on. They all knew she had other plans for the properties. Ones that would benefit her quest to run for President of the United States of America. What better favor than to give ocean front property to those that could help her the most, or sell for significant fund raising.

"It sounds like you have already made up your mind! Why do we need a committee if this is how things are going to be done?" asked the member with the original question concerning the lights.

"As for the lights, we do not need the committee. Like I said, everyone has failed to maintain them properly, and now it is a matter of public safety. Please have your reports on the other programs on my desk by the end of the week. Meeting adjourned." Capp briskly left the room.

12

Marilyn parked her car, grabbed her bag and headed for the dock. She really wanted to beat him to the boat this morning. What a morning. Bright sunshine warming the day every minute at this hour. She had gotten up early to get her supplies together, and to iron her outfit. She wanted to look professional the first official day of work in Maine. Not that she was thinking of being with Greg, or was she ? As she turned the corner down the pier where Greg's boat was moored, she spotted him on deck. Well, at least she was not late.

"Good morning Greg. Are we about ready to shove off?" Was that the right way to say it she thought.

"Yep." Greg said with a slight smile

"What, you don't like my nautical vernacular?" she asked with a bigger smile right back at him.

"Vernacular? Where are we? In English Lit class?" he quipped.

"OK. You got me on that one. A bit more, let's say, colloquial for you from now on?" she quipped back.

"Whatever. I hope you have a change of clothes in that bag. That outfit will look a lot more 'colloquial' when we get done checking pots."

"Confession. I do not know what checking pots is. But still willing to help. Do I need to run back to my room to change?"

"No. I have a suit you can use. It'll be a bit big but should keep you mostly clean."

"I'm game. When do we…leave?"

He smiled and said, "Right now."

They motored slowly through the no wake zone so not to disturb others in their boats and help prevent bank erosion. Marilyn was standing next to him soaking up the harbor views. Many different kinds of boats, and even more kinds of birds. Loud birds. No wonder everyone gets up early around here. As they left the harbor Greg pushed the throttle forward to set the cruising speed. With that, Marilyn lurched backwards not expecting it. He grabbed her around the waist and pulled her in tight to his left side, while she grabbed a hold of him at the same time. She looked up at his smiling face.

"You may want to sit down, it may get a bit choppy out here today."

She hesitated and stared, then said, "OK." She sat across from him, looking out over the ocean. She was thinking this may be an interesting first day.

They were headed for the Monhegan Island Light. Monhegan meant 'far away island' in Penobscot Indian language. The island was approximately ten miles from shore. It was the first landing point of most early explorers to the area. As a result there are many artifacts of those expeditions on the island. The station was originally established in 1824, and the lighthouse built in 1850. In 1959 the older Fresnel lens apparatus was replaced with a new automated twelve volt beacon system. This is used in over a quarter of Maine's lights now. Requiring little upkeep it was a popular model around the world. As they approached the island,

Marilyn gazed fondly at the forty seven foot gray granite lighthouse on the highest spot of the island. Then she spotted the red roofed innkeeper's house and museum adjacent to the light. Approximately seventy people inhabited the island, their well kept homes nestled in the hillside below the light. She thought this was the greatest job in the world. Focused on the lighthouse, those thoughts of Greg and his strong embrace were now second to the light. Greg dropped her off at the public dock and headed to check pots. He would come back by on his way back home to pick her up and check the last of his pots.

13

Marilyn was a little early for her meeting with the lighthouse keeper. The keeper was to pick her up at the docks to drive to the light and let her inside. There was a museum open to the public but the light was not, as with most lights. Some lights were opened for one or two weekends a year, so the public could climb up to the light observation area, known as the gallery deck, and get a better look at the lens in the lantern room. This was a big draw for tourists. She heard a voice from behind her.

"Marilyn?"

"Yes. I am Marilyn Barker."

"Glad to meet you. I am the light keeper and museum curator, Danielle Brown." She introduced herself

"Thanks for meeting me here to give me a lift to the light. Looks like a bit of a walk, and all up hill." Marilyn exclaimed.

"It is. We have a yearly run from the harbor to the light. Actually a walk for most of us. The hill seems to get steeper and bigger every year. How did you get to the island this morning?" Danielle asked.

"Greg dropped me off." she said as in passing.

"Oh, I see. You know Greg do you?" she asked with a big smile.

"We met at Pemaquid. I'm staying at the hotel there. He offered to take me to the lights on the islands. I guess he used to help the previous inspector, was it Guy?" she asked formally.

"Yes. Guy was great. But he never liked to be on the water. So he did not visit the island lights unless he really needed to. He retired to Kansas. Told me if he never sees another ocean he would be just fine with that. The lights were not his thing either. He actually just picked up the job to ease into retirement. He was an engineer for one of the big offshore oil companies. Was stationed on an oil rig for over a year he told me once, and he could not wait to get back on dry land." She explained.

"Well, I love the lights. So you will probably see a bit more of me than you did Guy." She said.

"Sounds great. Let's get going and I'll show you around the island then the light." She suggested.

Danielle drove the golf cart like a race car driver. The cart's engine had to have been souped up to move so fast. But she gave a thorough tour of the small island, including a place to stay and dine if Marilyn was ever stuck on the island due to bad weather rolling in while there. This was something she actually had not thought of. So, good to know! They ended up at the museum beside the light. Marilyn was excited to get started, but she followed Danielle into the museum for a tour there as well. By the end of the short tour Marilyn was glad they started in the museum. It was important to her to know as much as possible about every light, including their history. She had done her homework but Danielle covered things she had not read.

Danielle asked, "So, are you ready to see the light?"

A quick reply, "Yes. I sure am. This will be my first inspection on the east coast. It may seem silly, but I have been working for this for a long time."

"Then lets get you started." She said.

They walked to the back of the museum. Marilyn thinking why weren't they going towards the door they came in. Danielle opened a locked door leading them into a small brick building attached to the lighthouse. Probably best for when the weather was bad, but Marilyn wanted to see the light from outside as well. She would do so after the interior inspection. Danielle went back to the museum after showing Marilyn the basics. All lights are the same as much as they are different. At least that's what her father always told her. It took many years for her to understand that saying. Now it was part of the fun to find the similarities and differences between the lights, all while getting the work done. She had to remind herself at times about the work part. This lighthouse was in excellent condition. The care and upkeep was evident in every step of the inspection from foundation to top of the lantern house. The view from the gallery was beautiful. Monhegan Light was the second highest in elevation in Maine, just 2 feet less than the Seguin Island Lighthouse near Fort Baldwin in Phippsburg.   Standing on the gallery she gazed out over the mighty Atlantic as she had done the Pacific so many times. She looked at her watch, her father was definitely up. She wondered if he was working this morning. She took a photo of the ocean and sent it to him. Within seconds her phone pinged. She was looking at the Pacific on her screen. She had

to call him. They talked for almost a half hour. Both
were proud of each other and happy to have their
positions. It was a dream come true for Marilyn. They
said goodbye and she went back down to finish the
inspection.

After touring the grounds outside and finishing the
exterior inspection, she went to find Danielle for her ride
back to the dock.

"Hi Danielle. I'm done. What a great job you are
doing with the light and the property. Everything is
beautiful and in great condition. Do you do all the
maintenance yourself?" she asked.

"Sure do. Occasionally I need a third or fourth hand
and will call Greg for help." She said.

"Oh. Are you and Gregg…?" Marilyn paused.

"No. Or at least not any more. We were together
you could say for a while but things just did not
blossom, so to say. He's a great guy, if you're
interested." She suggested.

"I, ah, well, ah, am pretty busy, just starting out with
a new job." She stammered.

"That's not a no." Laughing, she went on, "Marilyn
you could do a lot worse than Greg. At least in these
parts. Not that you would just be settling for someone
with him. I miss, you know, being with him."

Marilyn smiled, with a slight blush on her cheeks.
"Maybe that is more than I needed to know."

"Don't wait too long. You have plenty of
competition out there, if you are interested that is."
Danielle went on to tell Marilyn more about Greg on the
ride back to the dock. By the time they got there

Marilyn felt she knew his life story and more.

"You two must have really been close to know that much about him." Marilyn exclaimed.

"In these parts we know that much about everyone. Our families, Browns and Smiths, are two of the oldest names in Maine. We used to kid around we had to be related somewhere in our genealogy. Yes, we had some good times... You better get going, the more we talk about him, I just may go after him again." She said with a smile.

Marilyn stepped out of the golf cart and thanked Danielle again, for everything. Marilyn had learned much more than she asked for. Then asked, "So, you think Greg would actually be interested in an outsider? I heard this area was not as open to outsiders as some places may be." She tried to say delicately.

"You don't have to try to be polite here, just say what you're thinking. You'll fit in better. And yes to both. We are more than a bit to ourselves and like it that way. And Greg would not have brought you here if he was not at least a little interested in you. Did he ask you to check pots with him yet?" Danielle asked.

"We are suppose to on the way back to the harbor. Why does that mean something?" she asked curiously.

"That is courting 101 for a lobsterman. And this quick in knowing you, he must really be interested. You are going to have some jealous Mainers looking your way. Just ignore them and act like you could care less about them. Which you should not anyway. Good for you, and Greg. But I want to know how things are going. You have to keep me in the loop. Let's get

together for dinner sometime. We can compare notes.
That will keep Greg on his toes. We can have some fun
with this." She said in a scheming way.

"I'm not sure that's the best idea." Marilyn said
sheepishly.

"Trust me, no problems. Greg is understanding and
fun. Let him know I suggested us meeting and see what
he says." Then she drove off like the green flag had just
dropped.

Marilyn walked down the dock wondering what she
had just gotten herself into. She had been thinking
maybe over time if things worked out…but now she felt
like the pressure was on. She knew for sure she did not
want to lose her chance with Greg. He was just pulling
up to the dock, after she had called him earlier. How
should she handle this, she wondered.

14

"Hello, is this Fred Davis?" the person on the phone asked Fred.

"Yes it is, who would be calling?" he asked.

"I would rather stay anonymous. I have some information that I believe you and your lighthouse friends would be interested in."

"Go on." Fred said curiously.

"Governor Capp is planning on decommissioning most, if not all, the lighthouses in the state. Then in turn claiming the land as state grounds, and giving or selling the land to individuals willing to help finance her run for the Presidency of the United States."

"How do I know this is true?" Fred asked

"You will have to dig for the proof. Try to get the most recent state budget meeting notes. You may have to file for them under the Freedom of Information Act. And you may tip off those involved by doing this, thus letting them know what you are looking for. If so, there will be fall out, and it may be directed towards you and your group. But if you do nothing, I am sure you all will lose everything." The caller hung up.

Stunned Fred sat back in his chair. This can not be true. How would she get away with it. Especially in Maine. There had been rumblings for decades that the lights could go away. That is why so many have worked so hard to keep them going. They had lost a few over the years, mostly to disrepair. It is just too

costly to rejuvenate them when they get too far gone.
This is why they had been so diligent the past ten or so
years to keep up on even the slightest problems and the
increasing regulations from the state to keep them open.
Unfortunately no matter how well they do, it remains
easy for someone to claim an over two hundred year old
structure is unsafe for use. He could not wait for the
next regular meeting. Fred picked up the phone to call
the committee officers for an emergency meeting along
with the attorney they had used in the past to fight
egregious state regulations. The attorney agreed with
the meeting and would file for the meeting minutes as
well as property rights and zoning laws for the light
locations. He would try to have everything for the
meeting.

15

Marilyn donned her given outfit, and unexpectedly it fit fairly well. This obviously was not one of Greg's. He must have a smaller first mate helping him at times. Then it hit her. Or a previous girlfriend, maybe even girlfriends, that he brings along with him. She would think a bit on how to play this.

"OK. I'm ready. What do I do now?" she asked.

Greg explained how to use the long hook to get the line under the orange buoy floating ahead in the distance. Then to put the line in the winch channel made for the rope. Turn on the winch to pull the pot to the surface. Turn it off. Then pull the pot onto the deck. Remove and size the lobsters, throw the culls back in the ocean and the keepers in the live well. Re-bait the pot and then put it back into the water. Reverse the winch until the trap is on the bottom and the rope becomes slack, then take the rope out of the winch and throw it and the buoy into the water.

Marilyn expressed about her newly learned trade with a, "Sounds easy!"

Greg warned, "Try not to get your glove caught in the winch, it will pull your fingers into the gears and take them off. That slows everything down."

"What?" she yelled. "You said nothing about missing body parts when you demanded I help you with your job."

"You didn't ask. Why do think so many pirates

have a hook instead of a hand?" he asked.

"They all got too close to Tick-Tock!" referring to the crocodile in Peter Pan.

"Such a city girl response!" he shot back.

"Really…and what do all the other girls you bring out here say?" she said with a smile.

"Why do you ask that? What kind of guy do you think I am?" he smirked.

"The kind that just happens to have a girl's outfit already on the boat. Surprised it doesn't have Danielle's name on it." She said not quite under her breath.

"Oh shit! What did the two of you talk about this morning?" he knew Danielle would spill the beans about him and have fun doing so. Not in a mean way, but just the same she would not hold back. That was just Danielle. And few people knew him better than she.

"Well, I don't have all my notes with me at the moment, but she is surely informative." Again with a smile.

"That's not fair. I barely know anything about you and now you know everything about me. What am I suppose to do now?" he said in exasperation.

"Probably ought to grab that line you are about to run over." She said.

He turned quickly, missing the line with his prop, but passing the buoy. As he made the circle to come back around to get the line this time, he said, "This is why it's much easier to do this alone. No distractions!"

"You can drop me back on the island. Danielle wants to meet for lunch sometime. Something about she has more to tell me. I'm sure it's about the lighthouse." She said in a devious voice.

"Get your hook and grab the line." He ordered

As she pulled the line in, a wave hit the side of the boat from the circle turn he made, lurching Marilyn towards the sea. Just as her feet left the deck, she felt the strong arm of Greg around her waist pulling her back on board. The second time he 'saved' her today. This time she was truly scared. She was sure she was gong in the water. Greg unhooked the line, dropped the hook, and turned her towards him, asking, "Are you alright?"

This time she held on to him tightly, her head buried in his chest. His arms were firmly around her as well. After what seemed to be minutes, she tilted her head up towards his, as their eyes met so too did their lips. The boat was adrift in the current. The two kissed, with the exploring passion only felt with a first kiss.

Finally he said, "It is a big ocean, but we can not drift forever. I need to get the boat back in line."

"Don't you have an anchor?" she asked.

As he thought how good of an idea that would be, his phone rang and rang. He finally answered it. It was Fred. A very excited Fred. He unloaded the upsetting news onto Greg. Marilyn could read his change in expression, and became concerned herself about what the call may be about. When Greg hung up he told her about the details of the call. Both were stunned at first. This was most definitely a mood changer. They would pick up later what was started. But for now they checked the pots as they discussed all that was running

through their minds. Asking all the what about
questions, and she can't do that because, and many
more. The return trip to the harbor was a somber one
for such a beautiful day.

16

The next morning Greg could not just sit around and wait for the special meeting to come up with a plan. Whether needing funds or to fight the Governor, both endeavors would require the same crucial component, the support of the people of Maine. Not only those along the coast but also the inlanders. They all benefited from the tourist trade. Some more than others. Greg decided he was going to go out and ask them their opinion on keeping the lighthouses in Maine. He would feel much better knowing he had most of their support before taking on the Governor. As he was leaving the light keeper's quarters he ran into Marilyn.

"What are you doing here this early?" he asked her.

"You caught me. I was going to break in, again." She said.

"Real funny. I don't need another bop on the head." He said as he smiled.

"I want to do my part to help. Without the lights I do not have a job. What can I do?" She asked.

"Well, actually, I was just headed out to get local opinion on the lights in general. Without support of the public we do not have a chance against the Governor. You can come along. Don't you have a light to inspect today?" he asked.

"No. I stayed up late to get my paperwork done on Monhegan last night. I emailed the report this morning. Everything was in order, so an easy report." She said.

"Hey, that may be helpful. Since you are the official inspector, it would only make sense that if you say a light is in good shape, it should be. And in turn the Governor's team could not decommission due to supposed safety issues. That would not be everything we need but most certainly a big point of support for keeping the light activated. As long as you are able to help us without getting in trouble with your boss." He stated.

"Technically, I am my own boss. Once commissioned by the federal government I am on my own. The act of making the commission has the forethought that the lights need to be continued and repaired. I just send in reports with what needs to be done. Get confirmation to fix, then send a final report when done. My recommendation has never been denied. If a light is in severe condition, then a justification study is done to determine the need to continue to operate a light in that location. If deemed not justified, then a hearing is setup to decommission the light. That is when public opinion is collected before the final decision. There are many lights that are still maintained due to public demand. Most of those are non working lights and are used for education, visual appeal and nostalgia. Some of these are sold to local non profits to takeover the care of the grounds and lighthouse. I have never seen a take over like what your Governor is attempting. She must have friends in high places or she will be surprised as to the red tape in decommissioning a light house." Marilyn stopped, looking at Greg's facial expression. He was obviously thinking of something as she explained her job.

"Marilyn, you said this was your first job on your own, correct?" he asked.

"Yes." She replied.

"Is this a typical first job assignment for an inspector?" He continued his questioning.

"No. Actually not. I had extensive time with my father as my apprenticeship, so to say, and with his reputation I feel it did get me an interview or two earlier than some with the same amount of time post graduation. I have always been up front with my schooling and never over sold my abilities." She defended herself.

"I am sure you are more than qualified for the job. Please don't take my question wrong. But if Governor Capp does have friends in high places, did they think they were getting a newbie for the position so to push you around when the time comes? They may not even know of your father, just that you are a relatively new grad applying for a job." He finished.

They both thought about the possibility. Is this actually bigger than they originally thought. A grand scheme worked out to the smallest detail so no one would be caught if an investigation were ever to ensue. Or, just an overzealous government official with a god complex thinking she can dictate without questions from anyone on how the state would be run. Marilyn did not have a history with Governor Capp, and Greg's was limited to what he saw on the news now and then. She had not interfered with the lobster business he knew that, and he had not heard anyone complaining about her affecting their business. Maybe they would however when they made their rounds today. They started in Boothbay Harbor, part of the heart of the tourist area.

Marilyn was fired up. How dare they try to play her. She was not going to just let anyone use her to get away with who knows what. As they entered one of the oldest stores in the harbor, and the state, Greg could see the fire in her eyes. The owner, a lifelong Mainer, face weathered over the years, was sitting at a desk a little ways behind the counter apparently doing the books. Marilyn introduced herself, the lady never looked up, and started on her save the lighthouses talk that sounded more like a tirade. It lasted all of ten minutes, describing what lighthouses were all about, their history, and why they were still needed today. Ending with, "…and I am sure we can count on your full support in these matters!"

After about fifteen seconds of silence, the lady calmly looked up, looked at Marilyn, then to Greg, then back to Marilyn, directly into her eyes, and with her authentic Mainer accent said, "Gregory, you can do better than this one." And then she was right back to her books. Marilyn heard the faint snort of a laugh coming from Greg, she turned with a mixture of what is with this lady and thanks for the support.

"Thanks for your support Mrs. Johnson. Have a great day." Greg said as he led Marilyn out by the elbow.

"Greg! What kind of support was that?" Marilyn asked as they got outside. "And thanks for the laugh of confidence in there!"

"You were right on, just about eight minutes too long. I know these people. If she did not agree she would have said absolutely nothing. And what you took as a dig, was actually just that. But she will give you another chance. Just not right now. Also, if she would have something else to say she would have. That tells me she has not been pressured by anyone, at least yet, to support the closings of the lights." Greg laughed a bit more as they walked to the next store.

The day was pretty much the same everywhere they traveled. Marilyn shortened her plea. Some owners asked what this was all about. They told them they were just making sure owners understood the value of the lighthouses for the local economy. Only a few did not seem to care or understand the draw of the lights and how the lights may be helping their business. There was no frank opposition, and that pleased them both. They went to dinner feeling they had a real chance in this fight. No matter which way it was going to turn out eventually.

17

Fred called the special meeting of the Pemaquid Light Society to order. He introduced Jeff Tileman as the attorney that had helped on previous conflicts with government regulations concerning Maine lighthouses. Some of the rulings had helped other states as well in regards to maintaining rights to keep lighthouses up and running, as well as open to the public.

"I have asked Jeff to look into any new regulations coming our way, or anything else he could find on the Governors plans. Go ahead Jeff."

Jeff began, " Thank you Fred. I will sum up what I have found and then answer any questions the best I am able." Jeff went on to explain that the lighthouse budget had been stripped down over the past ten years or so due basically to no complaints from elected officials. Overall there is just not the support among public officials when it comes to the lights. They all are trying to get their own, more modern regulations passed and are willing to take money from the lighthouse funds to do so. It goes back to the question, is it stealing if no one reports a theft? Most funding for lighthouses comes from private fund raising or grants. Grants may be private as well. Many ask for state and federal grant money also. There is no guarantee the grants will be renewed from year to year. It takes filling out all the forms and resubmitting each year, or time period set up by the grant, and hoping to get picked. Much like the corded telephone, lighthouses have been replaced by other more reliable and easier to use means of global positioning devices. "As for the Governors present plans, no one is sure. Everyone knows lighthouses are not on her priority list, they never have been. But there is no definite word of her actively trying to decommission any of them. The meeting minutes interestingly do not mention the light program at all. The land deals would be very difficult to get through zoning without much public commentary. She can promise all she wants, but delivering is another matter. I would suggest you continue what you have been doing. Garner as much public support for the lights as possible." He finished and asked for questions.

A member asked, "What about tenure status for lights?"

"Good question, I forgot to mention that." Jeff explained, "Tenure may protect teachers and professors, but as for structures, it is much more of an acknowledgment of importance than a binding agreement. At the time no one imagined not having lighthouses because they did not imagine anything being able to replace them. Again like the corded telephone. But today if I told you your cell phone would some day be implanted under your skin with audio and visual capabilities, most would say hard to believe but they could understand how advancements could make it possible. We have become used to the unbelievable in areas of computerized advancements especially."

Another member asked, "How hard would it be to get historical designation to protect the lights?"

Jeff answered, "Historical designation just prevents

federal or state construction projects from hurting the structure. The best choice is local designation so the local zoning board can try to prevent changes in the use of the land. This would make it difficult for someone to destroy the structure. But not impossible. That is why I believe the Governor will have trouble with the local zoning board. Again, there is no guarantee."

Fred asked, "If we petition the federal government to buy the structure we have to be able to keep the property up to public visitation standards, am I correct?"

"Yes." Jeff confirmed. "If a nonprofit is unable to meet standards of safety, then the local or state government may intercede. This would be the way I believe the Governor may try an end run, so to say, to gain control of the land. Then she would convince, or coerce, the members of the zoning board to let her rezone as she feels best for her needs. As you all know we have had to fight onerous safety regulations in the past. These are regulations that appear to be specifically focused on lighthouses as compared to other public spaces. Luckily the US Coast Guard tries to let non- profits take over the upkeep of lighthouses. However, we lose lights and the land to private buyers every year."

Greg spoke up, "We have the US Coast Guard inspector here today. Some of you have met her. Her name is Marilyn Barker. I would like Marilyn to let us know what her feelings are on the safety aspect of the lights."

Marilyn introduced herself and what her position

does for the USCG. "I feel most of the lights will meet my standards for safety and public use. However, there are federal, state and local standards. Since my reports are usually the only ones with engineering background, as well as experience with lighthouses, my report is usually used by all three to set standards and make decisions on the lights use. The Governor may try to have her own engineers dispute my report. I am willing to stand by my findings, even in court if need be."

Fred exclaimed, "There, we have it. The very person hired to inspect the lights. How can the Governor fight that?"

Jeff simply said, "Politics."

Though they all felt much better, they also knew they were not entirely safe. They decided to start documenting, even more, the use of the lights by the public to have proof of their use. Jeff would monitor the Governor's actions and talk with those he knew working in the different state committees that would be related to the lighthouses. Greg and Marilyn were to talk with a local advertising firm in regards to a save the lights campaign if needed. They would also discuss a proactive approach in trying to remind the public of the benefits of the lights. Other members would continue to monitor their prospective business associates concerning how they feel the lights support them. They all agreed lighthouse nostalgia and scenic beauty would not be enough alone to save the lights. The next regular meeting would be in approximately six weeks, hopefully they would not need another special meeting before then. That full member meeting would act as the official launch to save the lights from Governor Capp. They all did their part over the next month, gathering as much information as possible. Greg and Marilyn were getting to know each other better, but there was not another kiss. Marilyn was occupied with her lights, and Greg with his pots and the mission at hand.

18

Greg opened the door to his home and turned on the lights. It was early evening but dark clouds had moved in from the south making it seeming later than it actually was. He could smell the rain in the air. Probably going to be a storm worth staying in for the night. They had accomplished much the past month but had plenty to plan for the next meeting when all would be present. It was important to get everyone on their side and motivated to help.

"Cozy place. Does not reek of bachelor though, did you have some help, maybe a roommate to help with the decor?" Marilyn asked inquisitively and suggestively.

"Yes, we lived together for a short while. She added her touch to the place. After we decided to go our own ways I just left things the way they were, and still are." Greg said referring to Danielle, whom he was sure Marilyn was hinting about.

"That's nice. Something to remember her by?" she asked.

"No, nothing like that. I'm just not that in to redecorating. Even though it is small, just too much of an effort when I have better things to do." he replied defensively.

Marilyn walked around the house as if she were a prospective buyer. Opening doors to see what is on the other side, walking into each room, ending in the kitchen where Greg was heating up water on the gas range top in an antique looking kettle.

"Nice kettle. You like doing things the old fashioned way?" she asked.

"It was here when I moved in, and it works fine. So, when in Rome…" he said.

"Do you have any tea?" Marilyn asked as she opened a cabinet door.

"Are you looking for something? Other than tea that is." He asked

"No. Just interested in the person inside the man. I really do not know much about you!" she said, now defending her self.

"That's a bunch of bull. I'm sure Danielle told you everything about me." He shot back at her.

"Not everything. Did not have the time. That's why we are gong to meet for lunch sometime." She said with a smile. "Besides, without her intel, I wouldn't be here. Alone with someone, in his home, I know little about."

"Have you found where I keep my plastic sheeting, rope and meat clever?" he said with smirk.

"Exactly my point. Thank you for agreeing with me." She said as she approached him.

"I did? You were on a boat alone with me in the ocean. What about that?" he asked, turning towards her.

"You needed me to do the work. I had value for you to be kept alive." She suggested.

"Is that why I kept you from going overboard?" he asked softly as he put his arms around her lower back.

"I'm sure it was." She almost whispered as she

raised up on her toes to kiss him. This time no phone, but a brilliant flash of light from lightning followed by a tremendously loud crack, and then rumbling thunder. They both jerked their lips apart, still in each other's arms.

"What is it? Every time I kiss you we get interrupted." She asked.

"And even more impressive this time. That was close." He said in a louder voice. The rain was coming down hard now. The noise from hitting the roof and siding was growing.

"I am going to get soaked going back to the hotel in this. Do you have an umbrella?" she asked not really meaning it.

"No. I don't think you are going to need one." He whispered in her ear.

Reaching down he picked her up from just below her firm bottom. His hands fitting perfectly in the crease between her bottom and thighs. Her legs wrapped around him tightly holding her in place. Now eye to eye and lips to lips they kissed passionately, even more so than with their first kiss. His hands slid up to her back under her blouse. She reached down and pulled it off over her head as he unsnapped her bra. It fell between them as she put her arms down, this time to pull off his T shirt over his head. Skin to skin they kissed as he walked to the bedroom. Both were feeling similar yearnings and surging emotions. As he placed her onto the bed she laid back unsnapping her shorts, he pulled them and her panties off as her legs rose up to assist him. His pants fell to the floor and he stepped out of them into bed with her. Foreplay was not on either of their minds, nor needed, they directly engaged in passionate robust sex. They both reached their respective pulsating climax together. As they slowly declined melting together in a warm embrace, they were again interrupted. This time it was the shrill whistle of the tea pot. Neither knew how long it had been signaling, but they laughed as they lay in bed, bodies spent, listening to the pot calling them with the accompaniment of rain, lightning and thunder.

19

The harbor bar, pub, bistro, diner, all in one eatery was busy. Marilyn sat at her table sipping on a beer waiting for Danielle. Their schedules finally lined up to meet. They had kept in touch with an occasional text or phone call. Marilyn had inspected Nubble Lighthouse, the official name is Cape Neddick Light, earlier that day. Built on a nub off the shore of York, it is presently maintained by the city's park department. The island is just about a hundred hards off the bank, and the bank area is a great viewing spot of the light and grounds. There is a gift shop there also. Some claim it is the most photographed lighthouse in Maine, likely due in part that the parking lot is big enough to allow bus parking. Constructed in 1879, it was manned until 1987. That is when it was automated. Then in 1997 York was able to achieve permanent guardianship of the light and grounds, with the USCG still maintaining the light and horn. This was an example how a community is able to apply for guardianship of a lighthouse. With the light comes maintenance, which is where the fine print of any light contract is important. Who determines improper maintenance and public safety. As with any government contract, it is who you know not what you know. Nubble is one of the lucky lights. It is very popular with visitors and has great local support. Therefore, it was an easy inspection for Marilyn that morning.

Danielle waved when she entered, acknowledging Marilyn, then pointed to the back. As Marilyn turned to look in the direction of her point, she saw the restroom sign. Before she made it to the table the waiter brought Marilyn another beer and placed two in front of the empty chair across from her. Then left without saying a word. I guess they know Danielle very well here, she thought.

"Hey there. Nice to see you. Sorry I'm late. But that's island time for you. The ferry was late. I guess there was a cluster in the harbor this morning. Something about a youth regalia. Always thought those were crazy. Take a bunch of novice preteen and teen sailors, then set them loose in the ocean in a vessel they know little about. Maybe that is why Mainers are so tough. Learn to live, or die, early on. Speaking of living, how are you and Greg doing? Heard you spent the night last night!" Danielle downed the first beer between her sentences, pushed it aside and picked up the other with a big smile.

Marilyn sat there, with what she knew had to be a dumbfounded look on her face. She said, "How? It was just last night!"

"My second cousin works at your inn. She knows who's coming and going, so to speak. And with Greg and my history, well, just thought I may be interested." She said, with a playful smile this time.

"OK. Locals one, west coaster none. It was raining hard and I did not want to walk back in the rain. So, I just spent the night." She could see Danielle was not buying it. "And it was a very innocent night."

"How many times was it innocent?" Danielle asked pryingly.

After a bit of a pause, "Oh, what the hell. Three. Twice last night and once this morning."she whispered. "You probably know more about his love life than he knows himself." Marilyn almost shouted. She looked around as if to see if anyone heard her. Then laughed.

"There you go girl. Good for you. All work and no play makes for a dull life. I bet he made you breakfast this morning. Let's see… eggs, bacon, toast, and a cup of fruit. And I'd say you are a tea girl, not coffee." Danielle guessed.

"You have to have a camera in that house!" Marilyn exclaimed.

"No. Men are just creatures of habit. Rarely change things up. I could probably tell you how things went in bed, but as you know, I do not pry into others lives!" Danielle pronounced. They both laughed with that one.

Marilyn thanked Danielle for asking her to lunch. She did not know anyone on the east coast, and was a bit afraid of becoming a loner when not working. But she had actually been unexpectedly busy away from work. She was meeting many people and getting to know a few quite well.

Marilyn went on, "Even though my new best friend was my, I guess after last night, 'boyfriend's' ex, I think things are going quite well."

"By the way, I have not been able to find my favorite black pumps forever. I bet I left them at Greg's. If you find them, or anything else, let me know." Danielle asked.

"Sure. I'll just go through his house looking for all evidence of previous lovers." Marilyn suggested.

"I would. Actually I did. Didn't find anything though. The guy I am with now is getting serious. So I had to know if there were any skeletons in the closets." Danielle confessed

"That's great. Not the untrusting part, the part about getting serious. Do you feel the same?" Marilyn asked.

"Actually I do. And it's a bit scary. Never really felt like this. Even with Greg. Something was just different with this guy. Maybe because he was not from this area. I did not know everything about him and his family when we first met." She said.

"Nothing wrong with an out of stater is there?" Marilyn asked somewhat sheepishly.

"Oh, he is a Mainer! Just not from these parts. I am not dumb enough to go for someone from away." She said with a wink and a smile.

"From away? Is that what I am, from away." Marilyn asked

"Ayuh. But you are a good one. I can always tell. And Greg must feel the same. So if he is the one for you, don't let him go." Danielle warned as she raised her hand with two fingers up to the waitress signaling another round.

Marilyn said, "I'm going to need a ride back. And maybe help into my room."

Danielle was quick to respond, "I'll drop you by Greg's and put you in his bed. I still owe him one. You'll have to pay my debt. Ask him about it."

Marilyn laughed as she realized Danielle was serious. Oh boy, what had she got herself into she thought.

20

After Marilyn and Greg said their goodbyes that morning, she headed to Nubble Light and he to meet up with Fred and Jeff to go to the state capital in hopes to meet with an informant on the state budget committee. Jeff had been asking around and found someone willing to discuss what he knew about the Governor's plans with the lights. Lighthouses are a fixture of Maine, but many young Mainers do not feel the nostalgia of the lights. Change is inevitable but loosing your history along the way is unacceptable to most Mainers. Unfortunately, though it takes a majority to vote someone into office, after the election that person can take any side they want. They discussed many issues making the hour drive seem mere minutes.

Jeff had set up a meeting place in a private room of a restaurant who's owner was a friend and sympathetic to their cause. The informant wanted anonymity, at least for now, in fear of losing his position on the committee. Almost all governments have agendas that are kept from the public while in the working stages, then some purposefully keep secrets from the public. And some of these would be considered illegal. Where Governor Capp fell in this continuum was what they wanted to know. Was she using her office in an illegal manner for her own good. The three were early, so they got situated at the table in a back room of the restaurant, each with their own research notes, ready to meet the informant. They went over their plan concerning how to

question the person one last time. They were not sure
how cooperative the person would be. Jeff went out
front to wait on his contact.

A few minutes later Jeff and a young, twenty
something well dressed and strikingly attractive young
lady entered the room. He introduced her to them,
"This is Kelli Masters, she is an attorney and adviser to
Governor Capp. I will let her introduce herself with an
explanation as to why she is willing to talk to us today."

"Hello. As Jeff said I have a law degree. My special
interest is in environmental law. I have approximately 3
years experience post graduation from law school with a
large firm who specializes in that area.   I moved to
Maine from South Carolina. Thinking this would be a
good next step in my career and was promised to be
able to continue my special interest in environmental law.
It did not take long for me to understand that what
Governor Capp wanted was not my experience in
protecting the environment, but to use my knowledge of
doing so, to get around the legal barriers to gain state
control of the land. Over the past year I have settled
into the community, bought a house, met someone
special who works in the area, and not to mention is a
true Mainer, so does not plan on leaving." She said with
a laugh. "So I am committed to Maine also. Otherwise
I could just pack up and go on my way. I have
experience with lighthouses in the Carolinas. Though
Maine has more than both states combined. As you all
know the land they sit on is usually the gold mine rather
than the light, for the strictly financially motivated
person. And that person is Governor Capp. She is

basically a different person than I interviewed with. A true Dr Jekyll and Ms. Hyde. I have been around many like her working in the legal arena, but she is one of the best. I am somewhat embarrassed to admit she fooled me. That is another reason I want to make sure she does not get away with her plans, even if she is trying to do so somewhat legally. Since I am hired as a consultant and not as one of her counsel, I am able to discuss most of her dealings that are public matter. I was surprised she did not have that in my contract. Someone did not do their job, and I did not bring it up. I actually believe she was just going to use me for a few months then let me go. But she did not know how complicated it can be to take the land, even with what I have actually helped her with, sorry to say. Do you all have any specific questions?"

Jeff spoke up, "I am sorry to hear about your situation. Please tell Greg and Fred about her overall plan. I have not shared that with them yet."

She answered, "Sure, I assumed you had. In a nut shell, she plans on decommissioning all the lights that sit on usable land, be it for personal or business use. She is trying to find a way to then get the land to private citizens, most likely not Mainers, possession without breaking the law. These individuals will be the ones who help her most with her political aspirations. Though this may sound absurd, these type of favors happen all the time. Big money lobbying is no more than legalized bribery."

Fred asked, "What do the people of Maine have to say about this?"

Kelli answered, "Not much. She was just elected. So she has time on her side for now. Even if she goes all in she will not be worried about re-election here in Maine."

Fred followed with, "Can't we expose her plan?"

"That is what we need to determine. Is it possible to catch her in the act. Though she has stated her intentions, she has been very private in her means. I am sure her counsel is working on this. The information I gave them points out the hurdles in their way, but does not tell them how to get around them. They may be great attorneys, but if they are inexperienced in this area they will have trouble getting things right the first time they try. Then the plan should be exposed. But if it is not illegal then she is just hurt politically locally. Like I said she is not planning on re-election, she is planning on moving on out of the state."

Greg asked, "What is her primary basis of being able to decommission the lights?"

"Ironically, public safety." She said

Greg responded, "So the very public that put her in office, and wants the lights to stay, need protection from themselves?"

"Yes, exactly. And since Maine does not allow gubernatorial recall, she has four years to figure out what she is going to do." Kelli replied.

Greg asked, "What is our best way to stop or slow down her plan?"

Kelli replied, "Continue what Jeff says you are doing. Let the public know of your concerns. Try to convince the public of the need for the lights. And the most important person you have is the lighthouse inspector. If she is willing to go to bat for you, I do not see how the Governor can override a favorable inspection, at least legally. Because of that, your inspector will have to watch out for her job. I am sure Governor Capp will try to get the inspector reassigned once she realizes this."

Fred stated bluntly, "So you do not have a sure way to stop her then."

Kelli replied as bluntly, "No."

The drive home was a bit subdued.

"I guess things could have been worse. Capp could have already processed the decommissions. So we still have a chance." Greg stated.

Jeff responded, "Agree. But Governor Capp has friends in high places. We need to be careful who we trust."

Fred asked cautiously, "No offense Greg, but I have to ask, can we trust Marilyn. She was brought in from away, no one really knows her, could she be a spy for Governor Capp?"

"No offense taken. Good question actually. She has been very helpful. Let me check into that. Maybe I do need to keep a bit more of an open mind about her. Just like Kelli got fooled, maybe I have also." He admitted.

21

By the time Greg got home it was late. He went straight to his boat after getting back in town, and checked his pots. Good haul today. He got everything situated and put away before going home. He believed his boat and checking pots were much easier to get started the next time out if put away right. Some people left the clean up until the next day. As he walked into the house he could not get what Fred had eluded to off his mind. He had gone through all of his time with Marilyn in his mind, numerous times, while checking his pots. There was just no way she was a spy of some sorts. But did he really know her. He made up his mind that was the first thing on his agenda tomorrow. To confront her bluntly, and find out what she knows, and who she really is. He felt if he confronted her directly he could tell if she were lying. Besides, he had fallen for her. If she was working for Governor Capp he wanted to know as soon as possible so he could end things now. He had a broken heart well before he and Danielle were together, he did not want to go through that again.

As he entered the bedroom he noticed something was off. There was a lump in his bed. Under the covers. He did not always make his bed but this was more than just piled bed covers. He lifted the covers slowly and cautiously in the dim light coming in from the hallway, as if ready for something to jump out at him. Then he saw them, painted toenails. He peeked a little farther, she was on her left side, knees to her chest, head down, like trying to roll up into a ball. And she was out, dead asleep. There was just a hint of alcohol wafting from the lifted covers. He smiled. Danielle strikes again. There were few that could keep up with Danielle, and many that had stumbled home just to pass out after drinking with her. Marilyn certainly did not look like a spy at that moment. He put the covers over her body, leaving her head exposed. After getting ready for bed he slipped into bed, snuggling up to her back, his arm over her side and flexed legs. He closed his eyes for some well needed sleep.

Just as his mind was slipping into a peaceful slumber, he was jolted back awake by Marilyn's body springing back to life as she jumped out of bed. He laid there listening to the retching from the bathroom. Eventually it turned into the painful sound of dry-heaves. Then silence. Wondering if she fell to sleep on the floor, he decided to check on her but before he could he heard a moan and some rustling. She was moving about, flushed the toilet then gargled and brushed her teeth. She walked out of the bathroom, stood there naked and somewhat confused and startled.

"What are you doing here?" she asked.

"I live here." He responded holding back a laugh. He thought he better proceed cautiously.

She looked around the room, a dim light of orientation flickered in her face. "Oh, yea, that's right." She took two steps towards the bed, stopped, and ran for the bathroom again. Round two, of four. Each time she cleaned things up, followed by gargling and brushing her teeth. The last time, approximately three in

the morning. That time she felt good enough and
necessary to take a shower before retuning to bed. By
then Greg was turned the other way, sleeping soundly,
ignoring the events of the evening.

Beams of sunlight pierced through the center crack
between the curtains. Greg left them open just enough
to wake him if he were to sleep in. He usually was up
before sunrise, if only to sit outside and watch the
sunrise with coffee and beignets. It was something he
picked up while staying in New Orleans many years ago
helping a friend and learning the shrimp business. While
it was much different shrimping than lobstering, it was
similarly hard work to make a living from the sea. As he
rolled over he noticed the drunk alcoholic bum of last
night had transformed into a sweet smelling princess that
morning. He cuddled up to her back again this time his
arm going around her and his hand going up through her
breasts to the opposite shoulder. He gave her a firm
hug and then relaxed into her body.

"Not too hard. I do not believe there could be
anything left. But you never know." she said.

"You're awake?" he asked

"Habits do not change no matter how drunk you are
I guess." She moaned.

"I thought you got up early yesterday morning just to
take advantage of me. Something special. But I guess it
was just old habits?" he asked coyly.

"Hardly a habit. It was more than something special
also. Something exceptional." As she hugged his
muscular forearm. "I can not believe you saw, and
heard, me like that last night. I know I should be

embarrassed and should have crawled out of here last night but I just did not want to leave. Leave you. I hope you can forgive me." She softly pleaded.

"Nothing to forgive. Just another victim of Danielle. Hope you learned your lesson with her. Never try to keep up when she is drinking. Just say no." He warned laughing

"I almost forgot. She said I was to pay her debt. That she still owed you one? What's that all about?" she asked.

Without set up he stated, "Fred thinks you may be a spy for Governor Capp."

"Really. Just change the subject. And what do you think?" she snapped.

"Hold on, I said Fred brought it up. He was just looking at the time line. Shortly after you arrived is when we started hearing more about Capp's plans." he said defensively.

"I take it your meeting included conspiracy theories. Which means you did not find a smoking gun. So we, and yes I mean we, still have nothing definite to go on?" she asked more calmly.

"Not really. But the informant, Kelli, is in a good position to monitor Capp's' moves." He replied.

"Well that should be a help. And tell Fred you vetted me and I'm on your side." She exclaimed.

He rolled her over pulling her partially under him, "To do that I will need more examination of the subject at hand." His lips caressed her neck.

"Agree, but slowly and gently, at least to start this morning. I'll let you know when to move on…" her

voice drifting off as his lips moved slowly down her
body.

22

Portland Head Light is the oldest lighthouse in Maine. While Nubble Light is given the distinction of most photographed lighthouse in Maine, Portland Head is believed to be the most photographed in the U.S. Initially it had sixteen whale oil lights, and became operational in 1791. Later the light was replaced with a Fresnel lens, with upgrades that followed. Like most lights the ownership and care moved though a chain of government designations over the years. The Town of Cape Elizabeth eventually leased the property and cared for the grounds, and then through a local senator's support was granted the deed of the property in 1993. The USCG still monitors the light and fog horn. The previous keepers house is now an excellent museum. There is gift shop also, along with an approximately ninety acre park to explore. The grounds are run very professionally.

Marilyn spent some time in the museum waiting for her contact to get access to the light for her inspection. Even though she knew so much about lighthouses, it was common for her to learn something new when going through a museum like this one. She thought she would like to come back when she had more time to just enjoy the museum and grounds. The employee was apologetic for making her wait as he lead her to the entrance of the light. He offered to help in any way, as well as refreshments. Marilyn declined, she just wanted to get started. After last night she was not one hundred percent and a bit tired, but able to get her job done.

As she worked she could not imagine how anyone would be able to gain control over a light and grounds like this one. The grounds were historic in that it was here, before the lighthouse, that the locals waited in watch for the British back in 1776. But then again, the greater the history the greater the interest by collectors and those with enough money just to say they own whatever it may be. She had gone to an auction years ago on the west coast thinking she would pick up a few items for home decorations as well as the historic conversations they initiate. She was shocked by the amount of interest and even more so by the price they brought. And these were not what she would call museum quality pieces. She went home empty handed that day.

She stopped for minute while on the gallery to look out over the ocean. This would make for a great location for a dream house. Waking every morning with this view. If only she were one of the rich and famous, she could buy a piece of history to live on. As her mind wondered she eventually came back to reality. There was no way she would ever tear down a lighthouse to build a house, or anything for that matter. More so, she wondered how Greg and she could get every lighthouse this much public backing. She had decided to start with the better cared for lights, knowing there would be less angst in finding something that could lead to the demise of a light. Sometimes it may seem a very simple fix. But by the time it goes through the many committees for approval and then to find the money for repair, the light was in even worse shape. That is why she always tried to ask for enough to fix what is needed at the time and then by the time workers could actually get started. Some of the worst days of her job involved realizing a light's life was over. Knowing the money would not be granted for repair. The first light she recommended for decommission due to the cost of repair not substantiated by the need for the light was eventually torn down. She made herself watch the wrecking ball hit the structure over and over, then the bulldozer finish it off. She sobbed uncontrollably during the entire time. To her the lights were the U.S. equivalent to the great pyramids. And just like them, mother nature's toll eventually leaves its' mark. Without upkeep everything will decay away, some faster than others.

It was early evening before she was done and driving back home. Home being her hotel room. She was second guessing her choice of lighthouse due to her one and a half hour drive. Her stomach was OK, even a bit hungry, but she was tired. And what/where is she suppose to do/go? She spent the last two nights at Greg's. Now what? Are they a couple now? Does she move her things in to his house? Or are they friends with benefits? Life was easier when she just had her lights to think about. But as she thought about the last two nights, she felt it was worth it. She had to laugh as she drove thinking about the difference between the nights. The first was full of raw passionate sex, and the second raw ugly illness. She may not have the problem she had been worrying about, after all that Greg may have decided to move on. And could she really blame him. Show up unannounced, wait for him in bed, then barf most of the night. She jerked in her seat, startled by her phone ringing.

"Hello, this is Marilyn." She answered without looking who the caller was.

"Hello, is this Marilyn Barker." The caller asked.

"Yes it is. Who's calling please?" she responded.

"Ms. Barker my name is Beth, and I am a nurse at Santa Barbara Hospital…"

Marilyn's heart felt like it stopped. Her stomach was knotting up.

"I am calling with regards to your father, John Barker…"

Marilyn nearly shouted, "What happened, is he alright?"

"He is stable now, and should do fine. He had an accident at work causing a fall. He broke his right hip. The doctors are planning surgery in the morning. He is sedated now due to the pain. We do not see any other significant injuries. Your father asked that I call you to let you know he is alright and he will call you after surgery tomorrow with an update." Beth informed her.

"How bad is it? Should I come out now? Can they hold the surgery until I get there?" Marilyn asked in a rapid fire manner.

"It is not bad as far as breaks go. It should be a routine repair. I would not suggest postponing the surgery due to he will just be in more pain while waiting for the surgery. He should be out of surgery and able to call you by about six, our time, tomorrow evening." Beth assured.

"OK. You have my phone number. Please call with any changes. Tell him I love him, and…" Marilyn started to cry

"We will call with any change in condition or plan. He should do fine though." Beth said again in a reassuring tone.

Through her tears Marilyn said goodbye. She almost had to pull over but she wiped her eyes and kept going. She had to go see him. She wanted to get a flight but did not want to stop. She needed help. So she called Greg. Explaining the situation and asking him to search for a flight to Santa Barbara tonight if able. He called back in a few minutes. He got her information and told her she had a ticket on the red eye to LA then a car to the hospital, about an hour and half drive. Marilyn thanked him over and over. Greg reassured her everything would be fine. He would drive her to the airport as soon as she got back and packed.

They arrived at the airport in good time to catch the flight. Greg parked in the garage. They got out of the car and Greg got her bag out of the back of his vehicle. And then took another bag out.

Marilyn said, "What is that for?"

Greg responded, "It's mine. I'm not going without a change of clothes."

Marilyn teared up and gave him a tight hug. "You do not have…"

Greg cut her off, "I know. I am with you all the way."

They kissed and headed to check in.

23

"Code blue room 4218, code blue room 4218" was being announced overhead as Marilyn and Greg entered the hospital. Marilyn looked at Greg alarmed.

"I'm sure that is not his room. You said they would call if he had any change in condition. Let's ask for his room number." Greg said gesturing towards the information counter.

"Hello my name is Marilyn Barker, can you tell how to find my father John Barker. He broke his leg and is to have surgery today." She fired at the receptionist.

"Take a breath." Greg said calmly.

"Yes ma'am. Let's see. He is in room 3635. Use the elevators at the end of this hall," pointing to their right, "and go to the third floor. The room will be to your right. Do you have any other questions?" she asked politely.

"No. Thank you." Marilyn replied

Marilyn was getting emotional on the ride up in the elevator. As she stepped out onto the floor she burst into tears. Greg set the bags down and held her in his arms, letting her get the emotions out. She was scared. Maybe it was being away and starting a new life on her own. Something was different coming back to see him this way. When she came home from college it was always exciting. But now it did not feel like she was coming home. It felt like she had been away forever. Had her father aged that much in such a short time?

What could she expect? She did not want to think of him as elderly. He was always so strong. Her rock to lean on when needed.

"I am OK. Thanks. I just needed to get that out. Let's go see him." Marilyn said.

They walked down the hall, found 3635, and slowly turned into the doorway, and peaked around the curtain. He turned his head in bed and their eyes met.

"Oh my. What are you doing here? I'm fine." Her father exclaimed.

Marilyn went right to him and gave him a firm hug. A long hug, like she was never going to let go. Greg put their bags on a stand near the window on the far side of the room. John watching him as he walked around the end of his bed.

Marilyn started with her rapid fire questioning, "What happened? What were you doing? Why didn't you call me? I was so worried when the nurse called me. And…"

John put his finger on her lips, she stopped, then she smiled. "I still have the touch. Remember when you used to get so excited asking question after question, and I would do this?"

Marilyn nodded in agreement.

"And what would I say?" he asked.

"Look around and think before you ask. The answer is many times right in front of you. Don't let your emotions run away with your mind." She repeated for what felt like the umpteenth time.

"I have a broken hip. I feel fine, at least with whatever they are giving me. I was climbing up a spiral steel ladder inside a light, and a bolt, even older than I am, gave way from its anchor point causing the stairs to twist suddenly. I fell and hit my hip about two steps below where I was when it happened. The bolt did not actually break, but my hip did upon hitting the steel step. Occupational hazard. Something you can learn from also. So they are going to fix my hip and I'll be good as before in about eight weeks. It will be good to take some time off." he joked.

"You will still keep busy. No way this will stop you from working. You always have your consultant case reviews waiting for you from all over the world." Marilyn predicted. Now she fely much better seeing the same father she had left a few months earlier.

John then said, "More importantly, who is this guy. A man in your life. Now that is ground breaking news." He exclaimed.

Marilyn quickly replied, "Stop it. This is Greg. He is my…friend. Very good friend. Without him I would not be here."

Greg shook John's hand and said, "Glad to meet you. Marilyn has told me a lot about you."

"Really. She has told me nothing about you." John replied with a grin.

Again, Marilyn quickly jumped in, "Now Daddy you know I have been busy."

"Sure looks like you have." John said looking at Greg. John obviously was having fun with them. He trusted Marilyn with all her decisions, including who she dated. And John could tell already this was serious if Marilyn brought Greg with her, or let Greg bring her.

"Daddy we are just friends. Don't make more out of this than what it is." Marilyn said trying to deter him from going further. It did not work.

"So Greg, is that the way you see it. Just friends?" he asked.

"No sir. We are beyond just friends to be honest. Or at least I hope we are." Greg stated.

Marilyn now stammering, "Well of course we are, but…but…it's not like we are engaged yet."

"Yet!" John exclaimed. "Well now, I better get to know Greg here a bit better."

Marilyn had her head down in her hands, "Greg, I'm sorry. He is like a pit bull with a chew toy sometimes. And we really don't keep secrets. So, I'm sorry to you too Daddy. I should have let you know I met someone."

Greg was quick to chime in this time, "If there are no secrets should I tell him about your lunch yesterday and last night."

"Greg! I can't believe you brought that up!" Marilyn scorned him.

John laughed, "Now this is getting good. You two are a couple for sure! You better watch out Greg, she can get feisty."

"Maybe, but she can't handle her alcohol too well." Greg said laughing.

"Both of you are incorrigible!" she proclaimed loudly.

They both laughed this time. "Greg, I think you're stuck with her now." John said.

"I hope I am." Greg agreed, smiling at Marilyn.

"I wish I could get mad at you, both of you."
Marilyn said calming down after what Greg just said and
his smile.

Right on time the transport team showed up to take
John down to the OR for his surgery. They said their
goodbyes and see you after the surgery. John made
sure she remembered to bring her house key, not sure
what shape he would be in after surgery. He also
instructed her to go by the light where he fell and get his
vehicle for him. That should take care of everything, so
off he went. Smiling and happy that she made the effort
to show up, and even more so that he met Greg. There
always is a silver lining no matter how dark the cloud.

24

Marilyn opened her eyes slowly. They were still
blurry and accommodating slowly to the light coming in
through the curtains. She looked around the room while
lying in bed on her right side.   She could relive her
childhood looking at everything in the room. Posters of
many different lighthouses, models of lighthouses, a
piece of granite from a lighthouse in Oregon, ribbons
from school projects, mostly on or related to
lighthouses, a few sailboat models, one poster of a
young singer, her celebrity heartthrob one summer, a
basket full of teddy bears and a few other animals, and a
picture of her mother on the night stand next to her
lighthouse alarm clock. She missed her mother, even
though she only had a few good memories of her. She
always pictured herself being an inspector like her father.
But she never pictured herself lying in her childhood bed
with a man next to her. She reached back laying her
hand gently on his thigh. She thought since there was
no where to be first thing this morning they may as well
try to catch up on some rest. But with the time change
they both were starting to awake. Wafting in and out of
consciousness, tired yet the brain telling them it was
time to be up.

Her father did very well with surgery. He made the
two of them promise not to come back until after lunch.
They would catch up on rest, eat breakfast, then she
would show Greg some sights since they had her
father's vehicle. Afterward, they would head back to

the hospital. If all went well John should be able to go home the next day. It was odd enough lying in bed with Greg in her room with just the two of them in the house, what was it going to like when her father was home? Her father and she had a more open relationship than some of her friends did with their parents. He knew a young woman had yearnings as much as a man. She had come home very late and even the next morning a few times when she was still living with him. He took it in stride. He was always positive in his support but with a comment of concern for her safety at times.

She rolled over, gave Greg a hug and kiss, with plans to get up and get ready for the day, but Greg's arm around her was like a steel trap.

"Time to get up. Busy day." She said.

"Busy? John said not to come back until after lunch. What could be better than this? And I have a few questions about the items in this room." Greg replied.

"OK. What do you want to know?" she said as she snuggled in beside him.

"I want to start at the beginning." he said.

They spent an hour going over the life of Marilyn. Mostly they were laughing, some embarrassments and even a few tears. By the time they finished talking, they were kissing. Their recent bedroom escapades had been fun, but this was different. They embraced each other with determination and to understand the other beyond intimacy. This was a feeling understood only by two truly in love. They both understood that this time it was love. They finished, hearts pounding in harmony, as they caught their breath, and looked deep into each other's eyes.

"I love you." Slipped from Greg's mouth. He had never told anyone that. Even the girl that broke his heart. Probably because he did not feel as he did now.

"I love you." Marilyn replied with kept excitement in her voice. "I did not expect this so fast. From the first time we met, I knew you were someone special. You are the only person that has ever distracted me from my lighthouses."

"Interesting way to look at love. Enough to distract you. I guess I'm glad I was a distraction then. And hopefully will continue to be so!" he exclaimed.

Marilyn cautiously asked, "Where do we go from here? I have never been in this position."

"First, I think you were in this position a couple nights ago." He said with a smile.

She gave him a playful swat, "You know what I mean!"

"Second, either have I, so, I guess we figure it out together. I thought you were already a step ahead of me though, since you already moved into my house…" he said trailing off.

"And where are you right now. In my bedroom. So we are even. Sorta. Do you really think I moved into your house?" she asked

"Don't over think it. But you should, or I mean please do, or I mean I'd like you to, only if you feel comfortable with the idea" he said erratically.

"Now whose over thinking it?" she proclaimed. "And yes I would love that. I better tell Danielle before she hears from her cousin at the Inn."

"Small town charm, I guess you could call it. You can tell her that you paid her debt this morning." He said

"What was the bet in the first place?" she asked

"Danielle said she owed me one more time in the sack, as she called it, when we broke up for not being a douche-bag, her word, about our break up. I guess she had some bad experience in the past. We did not go into that part. Also, I know you wanted to get moving this morning. So thank you for opening up about your childhood and life." He said.

"You are going to make me cry. Let's get a shower and get moving. I want to show you some things in the area before we go back to the hospital." She said.

"Yes, Dear. Is that how that goes?" he said with a grin.

"Yes, it's the key to any great mar… relationship!" she said as she jumped out of bed. She grimaced as she walked away, due to her near mistake.

25

Kelli sat at her desk looking over the Governor's schedule. She noticed a recurring meeting every two weeks, that would occur on different days of the week. She had missed this in the past. But since the meeting was on the same day the past three times, it stood out to her. There were no notes or explanation of the meeting topic. This was odd. She wondered, could this be about her political aspirations including trading lighthouse grounds to get where she wanted to go. She knew the Governor kept detailed notes on everything she did. There had to be notes on these meetings as well. Kelli believed they were in her personal computer. The Governor would occasionally pull out her personal laptop to make or retrieve notes. Kelli had once asked her about the use of a personal computer with her government work. The governor simply dismissed Kelli's concerns. The next meeting was over lunch today. Kelli thought for a bit, should she call Jeff now, or investigate herself. She decided on the latter in case this was a just a dead end. But what to do next?

"Governor Capp I have those reports you asked for." Said Kelli. She waited until near lunch time to go into her office.

"Great. I'll take them. Good timing. I have a meeting over lunch that these may come in handy for it." Governor Capp replied.

"Do you want me to explain them to you. Or I can even give a presentation at your meeting if you want."

Kelli suggested trying not to show too much interest in her meeting.

"No. I'm sure I can figure them out. I will call if I have any questions. Just keep me up to date on any changes as we discussed." Governor Capp ordered.

"Yes ma'am." Is all Kelli said and returned to her desk. That did not work out Kelli thought. Now what? As she watched Governor Capp walk out of the office she was wondering how to find out where she was going. Capp's assistant had to know. Kelli rushed up to his desk.

"Jerry, I forgot to put one report in the binder I just gave to Governor Capp. She said she needed everything for her lunch meeting. Do know where she is going so I can get it to her?" she asked.

"Let's see. It's not in her schedule so she must be meeting with supporters. It is time for that. But that is a private meeting. She won't let you join them. I'll put it on her desk for her return if you want?" He stated

"What do you mean, time for that." She asked.

"Every two weeks. Gotta keep supporters happy. Without them there is no future, she is always saying something like that. Anyway, they meet in the back room of Harold's Diner. Looks good using a local establishment for meetings. Another one of her sayings. But she always complains about the food." Jerry went on.

"Thanks Jerry. Lets keep this mistake between us if that's OK?" Kelli pleaded.

"Know what you mean. She can be a bear some days. But you did not hear that from me!" Jerry said as

Kelli whirled around to get to her desk quickly.

"Jeff, this is Kelli. I have something for you. Governor Capp meets every two weeks with supporters. These have to be the people she plans on enticing even more support from with the lighthouse properties. And guess where they are meeting? Harold's back room!" she said excitedly. This was the same back room where they had met when Greg and Fred came to the capitol. So he knew the layout, and even more importantly, the owner.

"Good find! We can definitely drop by and overhear, shall we say, what she is up to. When is the next meeting?" he asked.

"In twenty minutes." She exclaimed.

"Damn. Let me see. No problem, I'll move that to this afternoon." Jeff said. "I am going there now and see what I can find out. Thanks again for the tip. This may be exactly what we need." he continued.

"Good luck!" Kelli got out just before he hung up. She sat back in her chair with a smile. There was no way Capp would understand the information Kelli had given her. So when Capp came back Kelli would have a chance to ask more pointed questions on why she needed the information Kelli gathered for the Governor. At this point Kelli would rather get fired than continue to support someone with Capp's motives.

26

Marilyn and Greg had a busy, productive and happy morning. Greg could better understand why Marilyn would light up when talking about her father and home. They drove around much of the Santa Barbara area with Marilyn pointing out sights and telling stories from her past. She could really get talking when she had much to say. Greg would just listen and watch as she would tell her stories. They arrived at the hospital after lunch as directed. They found John up in the hall ambulating with the physical therapist. He had more color and looked much stronger in just one day.

"Daddy you look great." Marilyn said while stopping his progress to give a small hug and kiss on the cheek.

"They say walking is the fastest way to recovery, so that's what I plan on doing." John replied.

"We'll wait in your room for you to finish. Take your time." Marilyn said.

"Sure thing. We are just about done with this session. I get to do stairs later today. So much to look forward to!" John said with some sarcasm.

Marilyn and Greg went into his room. Looking around she found her father's glasses and cleaned them. Her daily duty as a child now was just habit. He would let them get so dirty, especially after being in some of the unkempt lighthouses, that it would bother Marilyn more than him. She rearranged his magazines and put new ice and water in his hospital issued cup with bendy straw. Finally she sat down beside Greg. He had been watching her intently.

"So, were you a caregiver in a previous life?" Greg asked

"No. Candy striper. I entered the youth volunteer program with a friend of mine one summer. She was very interested and I just went along for something to do with her. I did learn very much about the little things that make a patient feel better during their hospital stay. And most importantly I learned that no matter how hard you try, some people just feel better being grouchy. That was OK too. I just kept doing my job and let them complain about whatever was on their mind." She replied.

"Obviously that did not sway you from your career with the lights." he stated.

"No way. I never thought about or wanted to do anything else. I can not see my life without lighthouses…" she paused, "or without you now." She said in affirmation.

"You do not need to wonder any longer. I am here to stay, if you'll have me." Greg proclaimed.

As she was thinking was that a proposal of sorts, her farther rolled into the room in a wheelchair, the therapist trailing behind.

"Finally done, for now. Have another session later today. So what'd you guys do this morning?" he asked

"Why are you in a wheel chair? Do we need to build a ramp at home?" Marilyn fired.

"Take a breath. Just need to learn how to use one. I do not plan on needing it but it's all part of the rehab.

Right Linda?" he asked.

"That's right Mr. Barker. You are doing great. I do not think you will need one." Linda agreed. She was his physical therapist.

"OK. But if you need one we can…" Marilyn started but was stopped by her father's raised hand.

"I know you will move heaven and earth but I am fine. If I need help I can call someone. I do have friends you know." John reminded her.

"That's not what Marilyn said earlier. Something about not having anyone to care for you but her." Greg said with a wink.

"Do not get started with that. Both of you just stop. I am going to get something to drink. Would anyone else like something?" she asked sternly as she walked from the room.

Neither took her up on the offer. And Greg stayed in the room with John.

"So, Greg are you sure you can handle…that!" John exclaimed with a raised hand towards the door.

"I'm sure. In some ways we are still getting to know about little differences but we are on the same page most of the time. Actually more than anyone I've ever known." he admitted.

"Sounds serious. Anything I should know?" he asked

"Actually, yes. I do not want to lose her. I am not sure when, but I plan on asking her to marry me. With your blessing I hope." John professed.

"I was actually kidding. But I can see you are serious. We do not know each other well but I do know Marilyn, probably better than anyone, so far. And I know she is in love with you. She has never been so attracted to anyone. If you are serious about her and she about you, you have my blessing. I even have something for you. We'll talk more when I get home." John said.

27

Greg's phone rang while he and Marilyn were driving back to John's house.

"Hello Jeff. You are on speaker with me and Marilyn. How are things going?" Greg answered.

"Great. Actually better than great. Kelli really came through for us. She discovered an off the official books meeting Governor Capp has been having every two weeks with different supporters as she has been garnering support for her future political aspirations. She has actually been able to attract some very wealthy individuals. She is a shrewd business woman, I have to give her that. The best part is that she chose Harold's as her local meeting spot. With my connections I have been able to listen in on her last meeting. All legally mind you. Luckily shrewd does not mean always smart. I think it is the arrogance in politicians that they feel they can do what they want and get away with it that makes them make mistakes. Meetings of this nature should be done in a much more secure place. Sorry, I digress. She has basically put some of the light properties up for sale. Call it lobbying, but it's still actually bribery. She put a starting dollar amount of support on six light properties, and is planning an auction of sorts. Highest bidder wins." Jeff paused for a response.

Greg responded, "We knew she was trying, but listening to you lay it out like that is amazing."

Marilyn spoke up, "It gives me chills."

Greg asked, "Which six is she going to start with?"

"I am working on the list. She is sending out a confidential list to only those who support her at a certain level thus far. Which means if you want to see the list you have to pay up front. Again, very shrewd of her. Like bidding up the pot hand by hand in poker, just enough to keep everybody in the game so you will make the most in the end, when you know you have the best cards. Kelli said she is going to push on her end to try and get the list also. She may lose her job pushing too hard, but we have the information we need to take on the fight with Capp at this point. Anything else Kelli can get will just make things easier, but not necessary. Kelli does not want to do anything that would end up strengthening Capp's position. Yet she does not want to lie and be the scapegoat for Capp when this all becomes public. Kelli can stand by all the research she has done under the guise of the safety of the lights, not to sell off the land for Capp's benefit." Jeff finished.

"Sounds like we need to meet again to decide our best strategy from here. Do we take this to the full meeting or do we need to prepare something for the group?" Greg asked.

"I feel between what I have and Kelli may come up with, I am ready to present to the full group. Besides, Capp is pressing forward with this so we do not want to get too far behind. We may not be able to stop her if she gets too much momentum." Jeff stated.

"Marilyn and I are in California, we will be home by the next meeting, so let's plan on exposing Capp then. Fred can put it on the agenda and see what everyone

thinks about this. Hopefully, they all will be as appalled
as we are." Greg said.

"Agree. Will be in touch. Goodbye." And Jeff hung
up.

They were pulling into John's driveway when the call
ended. They got out of the car and walked into the
house without saying anything, letting the conversation
settle in their minds. Then Marilyn spoke first.

"This is awful, really scary. What would happen if
the lights were gone? What if Pemaquid is on the list?"
she asked.

"Agree, but nothing is forever. We do not see many
horse drawn buggies or land line telephones anymore.
Both the mainstay of their times. I am sure many
thought they would never be replaced by the modern
alternatives." Greg replied.

"Are you saying to give up, or it's too late, it's
inevitable?" She exclaimed.

"No. But the lights are not used for their original
purpose. At least not primarily. GPS is the modern
alternative, and much more informative and reliable
actually. If we took every light down today, how many
people would be affected by that. Not many. Most
would not even notice in their day to day lives." Greg
said. She agreed but said nothing for a while.

"What else can we do?" she asked.

"Continue what we started. If we can remind or
convince the public that the light program is worth
keeping then we have a chance. Even if Capp does not
need to worry about re-election in Maine, bad press can
hurt her chances of being chosen to run elsewhere." He

declared.

"Sounds good. It looks like Daddy should be OK here alone. And I know he is not alone. He has many friends. So we can go back after tomorrow. We probably should get flights arranged." She said with some remorse.

"I agree he is doing great. We can stay as long as you want, and come back any time. But if you tell him about our lighthouse problem, what do think he is going to tell you?" he asked.

"I know exactly what he would say, get back there now and fight with all you have to save those lights." She said.

" You know him much better than I, but I whole heartedly agree. He is a great guy. We ought to have him come out to stay with us when he can travel better." He suggested.

Marilyn just smiled at first, "With us? That sounds nice. The past few days went from wonderful to horrific to hectic to tentative to wonderful again with that simple suggestion. I never even thought of that. Our relationship feels like it has wavered from a few days to forever in such a short time. But I like the forever side of it." She said.

"We will get him home tomorrow and settled in. Run our new proposal buy him. And I would like to get his input with our light situation. He is extremely well versed in the plight of lighthouses, I am sure he will have some helpful suggestions. Before he kicks us out to go back and fight." He said, and they both laughed at that.

28

The next morning John was discharged home. He was to follow up with out patient physical therapy. They got all his things together in his room and were waiting for the transport person to wheel him down to the car. Small talk was waining so Marilyn brought up their plan.

"Daddy, Greg and I would like you to come stay with us for a while once you are done with physical therapy and moving around easier." She said.

"With us? I take it you are living together now?" he asked.

"Well, yes. Or we will be by then. I mean…" She stammered a bit.

Greg chimed in, "What she is so eloquently trying to say is, Marilyn will be moving in with me when we get back. We will have plenty of room for you, and would enjoy your company."

"Yes, that's it." She confirmed.

"Well now, the surprises just keep coming with you two." John said with a wink towards Greg. "Marilyn runs off to Maine, now she's shacking up with the first guy she finds. I thought California was liberal but Maine may have them beat!" he said laughing.

"Daddy. You know I would not…" she started to say.

John said cutting her off, "I'm happy for you. For both of you. And I would like to see Maine. Even spend a day or two with you guys, if we have time."

"Oh, we will make time for you. Just let us know when you will be coming." she was quick to respond. Then looking at her father's face she realized he meant we as in he and someone else, not we as in Greg and her. "What did you just say, or mean?"

The transport guy came in to the room asking if everyone was ready, and Marilyn gave him the finger, the index finger, as in just wait a minute there buddy.

"We can talk about this later. I do not want to keep this fine young man waiting." John said with a big smile.

"Daddy! I came all the way back home, have been here for two days, and am just now hearing about WE!" she exclaimed

Greg headed for the door to go pull the car up.

"It's not too late to run Greg!" John shouted as he got into the wheelchair.

Greg laughed loudly as he left.

"This is not fair or funny. You two…does he know about WE?" she said, changing her thought in mid sentence.

"No. And you are not going to either until you calm down. To the car sir." He said to the transporter.

It was a quiet ride home. Marilyn was processing things in her head. She wanted this for her father. Even encouraged him along the way. So she was happy for him. But she expected to know about it from him when it happened. Then she realized that she had not been as open with her father as maybe she could have been. And that, did she really want to know everything? She sure was not going to tell her father she had sex in her old bedroom with Greg. And how far had her father gone with this person? No, she did not need to know that.

"OK. I am done processing things. Just like you used to tell me, think it over before you react. And I am very happy for you. You should know that. It was just a shock, with everything that is going on I guess my emotions are on edge. So will you tell us about her?" she asked.

"Sure. Probably to little surprise, I met her while inspecting a lighthouse. She was there to photograph the light for a magazine I thought. She took what seemed like a hundred photographs. I kept moving along my inspection to try to get out of her way, but she just kept following me. Finally I told her I was done and would be leaving the light to her, when she asked me if I wanted to get something to eat. I agreed. We went for lunch. She asked so many questions about the light, it actually reminded me of you. By now I'm thinking this lady is really special. She is interested in the very thing I do and love every day. As we finished lunch I was ready to ask her out on a date, but before I could, she says thank you very much for the interview. Confused, I just asked her what are you talking about? Interview? She looked at me, now her turn to be confused, and asked me didn't they tell me she was there to interview ME for the article. The article was not about the light but about me, the light inspector.   About then we both understood each other's misunderstanding of the lunch. I took it as a date, my first in along time, and her as just another work interview. We laughed, and have been seeing each other every few days since." He finished with a reminiscent smile.

"That's a great story." Greg said.

"How long have you been seeing her?" Marilyn asked

"Now don't get mad, but just over four months." He said cautiously.

"Wait. That means you were seeing her before I left!" Marilyn exclaimed.

"Yes. But I was not sure it was going to amount to anything. Until after you were gone. Then you had so much going on with a new job, I did not want to worry you. So I guess we both had a surprise brewing for the other." John said confidently.

"Well, where is she? I would think she would have come to see you." Marilyn asked confused.

"She is on her way back from Arizona. She was visiting her grandchildren. You know what those are hopefully!" he said with a smile.

"Yes Daddy we know." Marilyn said shyly. "What did she say about the fall and injury?"

"I'm sure she will be concerned, and sure she will help out where needed." John said shyly in return.

"FATHER. You did not tell her yet, did you?" Marilyn demanded.

"No. But I told her you and Greg surprised me with a visit. And she is anxious to meet both of you. She should be at home when we get there." He advised them.

"What. I am not dressed to meet anyone. Especially your girlfriend. Oh, that sounds…different."

She practically shouted.

"She's not anyone special. Well I mean you don't have to get all fancied up to meet her. Just try to be yourself." He encouraged

Greg quipped, "I think this is going to be fun. Watching both of you squirm like a worm on a hook."

"Not funny." John and Marilyn said simultaneously.

29

As they neared John's driveway they saw a vehicle parked on the left side.

"Is that her car?" Marilyn asked anxiously.

"Yes." John replied. "Let's just stay calm through this. OK?"

"OK. But you have more to worry about than we do. If I were her, I would be quite upset you did not tell me you were in the hospital." Marilyn warned.

"I'm beginning to think that may have been an unwise decision. I still stand by my belief that there was nothing she could do and no reason to worry." John tried to convince himself.

They were out of the car, John on his crutches, and headed for the front door when John's girlfriend came out and met them. The crutches were an obvious give away that something was up.

"John, what is this? What happened? Are you alright?" she asked.

"Everything is fine. Just a little fall. I will be good as new in a few days." John said. Before he could introduce his girlfriend Marilyn spoke up.

"More like a few months!" Marilyn exclaimed. John shot her a stern look of disapproval. "What? You already lied to her, in sorts, there is no use adding on to that."

"What is going on?" she asked.

"OK. It is a bit more than I led on. I fell and broke

my hip. I did not want to worry you. And yes, I am doing fine and will be even better in a short while." John said. "By the way, this is Shari, and this is my big mouth daughter Marilyn and her boyfriend, Greg."

"Nice to meet both of you." Shari said as she shook their hands. "And I think we will need to talk more about this stubborn old codger." she said to Marilyn with a wink.

"You really do know him well." Marilyn said with a laugh.

"I think you're in trouble." Greg said to John.

"My leg hurts. I need to lie down." John said meekly.

"Do not think that playing the "poor me, I am hurt" card will get you out of trouble." Marilyn warned.

"I agree." Shari said. "Why do men think women can not take hearing the truth?" she asked.

"Yep, you're screwed." Greg said

"I'm liking you less Greg." John said as he slowly sat then laid on the couch.

"Now he does not want to hear the truth." Shari said. "But, I still love him, stupid as he can be sometimes." She followed up.

"That's nice. I think?" John said.

"Do not let him get the best of you. You should be upset with him." Marilyn said.

"I will not let him forget. I am glad you came to help him. Such a long way though. Are you staying for a while?" Shari asked.

"Unfortunately we have to get back. And since he will be in such great hands, I do not feel as bad leaving him. Daddy we have something we want to discuss with you." Marilyn said.

"Let me guess, you're pregnant." He snickered.

"No. Don't be silly." Marilyn said.

"Well you show up with a guy, tell me your living with now, what's next? And I think that would be great!" John exclaims.

"Actually John, it is about a problem we have concerning saving our lights back home. Seems our Governor would like to decommission, on grounds of public safety, some of the lights, if not all, to gain control of the land. Then she wants to make arrangements for large donors to her political aspirations to obtain ownership of the property. We are trying to get public support for the lights then will try to block her intentions any way possible. We were hoping you may have some suggestions for us." Greg explained.

"Now this is very serious. And it can be extremely difficult to stop once the wheels are in motion. So it's best to try to stall early as possible. Make it hard and expensive for her to move forward. Also, find out who the supporters are. They many times do not want the bad press. They may have more to lose with bad press than your governor does. I have seen this happen over the years. Usually kept very quiet, then all of a sudden down goes the light and up goes a mansion. She can certainly make a bunch of money that way." John explained.

"Daddy do you mind if we leave tomorrow. There is a flight out in the morning." Marilyn said sadly.

"I expect you to do whatever it takes to save those

lights. You probably should not have wasted the time coming to see me. Though I am glad I got the chance to meet you Greg. Since this is our last night I suggest we all go out for dinner." John proclaimed.

"No!" Marilyn and Shari said simultaneously, then laughed.

John just shrugged his shoulders, "I tried. How about take out then. We will have a nice dinner here tonight."

"Better yet I have plenty of time to make a meal. Marilyn and I will run to the store, while you two talk about whatever, and then we all can help with the meal. It will be a great time for us all to get to know one another." Shari suggested.

The others agreed. And while the ladies were at the store John gave Greg a family heirloom. He told Greg that Marilyn's maternal grandmother and mother both used the engagement ring. When Marilyn's mother died he kept the ring hoping he would have the chance to give it to her expected fiance. Her mother used to say she would gladly give it up when the day came. John hoped this would help Marilyn with her mother not being here. He told Greg he could redo the ring, but Greg told him it was perfect as is.

They all had a great evening together. The next morning there were tears but they all knew it was time. There were also plans discussed of John and Shari coming to Maine in a month or so, dependent on John's rehab. John wanted to be kept apprised of any new developments in the case of the Maine lights scandal, as he dubbed it. Marilyn liked Shari very much, so much so, that leaving her father this time was much easier knowing someone would be with him. She was so happy to see how well they got along. She watched them waving, as she and Greg drove away, and she could not help but think where she and Greg would be when their age. But first, she needed to move in with him when she returned. Then, let the journey begin.

30

It was evening by the time they made it back to Greg's place, now their place. Marilyn went to the hotel and checked out. She avoided saying where she was going. Just that it was time to move, alluding it was due to her job. She wondered how long it would be before Danielle called. She did not have to wonder long. Her phone rang before she made it the few minutes to the light keeper's home, now hers. This would be the closest she had ever lived to a lighthouse. Certainly the next best thing to actually living inside the light.

"Hello." Marilyn said.

"When I told you not to wait too long for Greg, you didn't! Moving in, now that is bold. I guess that night I dropped you off things went very well!" Danielle exclaimed.

"This is amazing. Your cousin should work for the FBI or CIA. She is quick. I am just now pulling up to the house!" Marilyn exclaimed back.

"What can I say, small town and nothing else going on. Your love life is the best thing going. I did hear that someone is going to have a baby soon, so you may get bumped off the top of the gossip train." Danielle predicted.

"I can only hope and pray for that. And that the baby is healthy." Marilyn said.

"More gossip if not." She replied.

"Danielle! That is awful!" Marilyn shouted.

"I don't mean anything bad. Maybe just ugly, or an extra toe or something." Danielle said wishfully.

"You certainly look at life your own way." Marilyn said laughing.

"So, what's the scoop. You two getting engaged soon?" she asked.

"No. I don't think so. Just moving in together." Marilyn said.

"You don't seem like the moving in together type without a commitment." Danielle expressed.

"What do you mean by that? This isn't my first relationship." Marilyn responded.

"Bet it's the first time you lived with someone. A guy that is." Danielle shot back.

"Well, yes…but that does not mean anything. Just not the right guy in the past." Marilyn said defensively.

"You two are in this for the long haul. I just know it. So get ready Mrs Smith, it's going to happen." Danielle predicted again.

"That would not be so bad. Would it?" Marilyn asked.

"No. It would be great for both of you. And me!" she said

"Why you?" Marilyn asked.

"Think about it. You don't know anyone in Maine better than me. That makes me the maid of honor. And your bachelorette party will be epic!" she said laughing.

"I do not think I would survive. But you will be my maid of honor. What am I saying? We are just living together. Do not spread rumors of more than that. As a matter of fact do not even tell people we are living together." Marilyn said.

"Too late. Everyone will know by tomorrow. Not just by me mind you. But Greg is too well known for this not to spread fast. Just go with it. I take it you're not ashamed of the situation. Some will resent you, being from away, but most will accept you more because of it.   Now if you go and hurt him, then you may want to leave the state." Danielle said with a chuckle.

"I am certainly not ashamed. And I will never hurt him no matter what happens. So I guess I will just have to embrace the way things are done around here. I had not thought about any fall out publicly from this. Thank you for the warning." Marilyn said.

"That's me. Always looking out for you. Keep your head high and smiling. You'll do just fine." She advised.

They said their goodbyes and Marilyn took her first load into the house. Greg came to help with the rest. He asked what took so long. She just said Danielle called, and that was all Greg needed to know. He was glad they were friends. He knew Danielle would help with the adjustment to Maine life. She did not have that much but once they started moving this and that to make room, that led to moving more this and thats and before they knew it, it was two in the morning. The house had a make over, and a list on the kitchen counter of everything needed to finish the transition. They were both too tired to go on, and Greg too tired to argue with any changes, not that he really disagreed with anything, so it was time for bed. The first night together in their house now. Both were asleep within minutes.

31

The next morning Marilyn and Greg were on the water early. Greg had taught Marilyn how to run the boat while he checked the pots. After she almost went overboard he felt she would be safer driving. It may be safer but it was more challenging many days. She had to get the boat in the right place for Greg to hook the pot line below the buoy without getting the line tangled in the propeller or rudder, and keep the boat in the same position. Dependent on how rough the sea was and/or tidal currents the boat could move quite a ways during the short time Greg would check the pot and throw it back into the sea. It was important to keep the pots where they would best catch lobsters. Greg understood the bottom terrain and where lobsters liked to live, so the places he picked were not just at random. Marilyn was still learning that part. So she just tried to make sure the pot went back down as close as to where it was when they brought it up. She was up for the challenge and enjoyed being out on the water with Greg. The two had turned into a good team, cutting his time to check the pots by about thirty percent. Every time out Greg would have to instruct Marilyn less on how to do her job, and she could anticipate better what Greg would want to do next. She was a lobsterman in training and proud of it.

They made it back to the harbor in time to take care of the lobsters and boat before heading out to get caught up with the latest developments in the Maine lights scandal, as dubbed by John, with Fred. As they pulled up to Fred's place Greg noticed Jeff's car there also. At first he thought they got lucky but then figured it may mean trouble. Jeff would not be there unless there was something going on, most likely a problem. They walked around back to Fred's large deck looking out over the ocean, it was the meeting place. Greg knew he would find them there. They were surprised to see Greg and Marilyn. They both asked about Marilyn's father and were glad to hear things were going well. With that they then turned to the topic at hand.

"Why don't you bring them up to speed." Fred suggested to Jeff.

"Sure. Governor Capp has done it. She decommissioned an island lighthouse that no one has used for years, and is practically falling down on its own. It is not even on the list of Maine's lights any longer, but still is officially a light with the USCG. We feel this is a test case. It is still not public. We are not sure when, if ever, that will be announced. Kelli called me to let me know she had received an email meant for Capp. Since it was sent to her she read it before forwarding it on to Capp. Kelli believes this may be the end for her now that she knows what is going on. We were hoping Marilyn may be able to find out more about the light and grounds with the USCG. But that is not the bad news. No one will miss that light, most probably do not even know it is on the island. The email Kelli received had a list of other lights of interest. The next on the list was Pemaquid." Jeff explained. Silence followed for a few seconds.

Greg spoke up, "Pemaquid. That's amazing. I never imagined she would try this with a well known light. How does she think she would get away with this?"

"It's not about the light, its the property. There is plenty of land there for a large house, a mansion, with a great view. My guess is one of her donors has picked the spot. As for getting away with it, she will not be around to deal with the aftermath. Her plans are to move on, out of the state." Jeff replied.

"That light is in great condition, and still in active use!" Marilyn exclaimed.

"They probably will keep the light working. The new owners may want it on the property for its charm. It may be why she is entertaining the option. Not as hard as decommissioning the light, just needs to take control of the land. And if the new owners are willing to pay for the light's upkeep, she just saved the people of Maine money. She may spin this as her way of saying thank you to the people before she leaves her office." Jeff surmised.

"The new owners aren't going to allow people through their gates to see the light, are they?" Fred asked.

"Well no, not at all. That part will not be discussed, I'm sure." Jeff replied.

"I never thought of this." Marilyn said, and went on, "It is actually very clever and devious all at the same time. That would basically cut out the USCG's expense of maintenance. They still have a functioning light. The cost of ground and light maintenance would be covered as long as the responsibility is added to the property deed. I would still be able to do my inspections. The only thing different is the lack of public access. And as long as she can claim public safety as more important than public access, she goes off to wherever as a hero of sorts. Saving tax dollars without losing the lights."

"The general public, especially the youth, just do not care about history. Everything is new and changing so quickly that no one expects anything to stay around long. Newer is better. They line up around the block for the next generation of whatever is coming out next. Historical societies are becoming as antiquated as the relics they so desperately strive to save." Fred said.

They sat in silence for a few minutes. They were all letting things sink in. Then they were trying to figure out a way to save themselves along with the lights. For Greg, and now Marilyn, it would mean moving. For Fred it would be the end of the Pemaquid light society, and for Jeff it would mean a loss in his legal fight to try and maintain historical sites. They all believed in the mission before, but now it was truly personal. The fear was becoming palpable as they sat there feeling like they were just hit in the gut.

"It's time. We have to expose the Governor's plan. Then hope and pray we get a public response that she will have to listen to. It is our only chance. Do you all agree?" Greg asked

They all nodded. A plan was devised. They would start in the morning.

32

Kelli sat in the meeting room alone. She had been summoned by Governor Capp through the Governor's aid. This is usually not a good thing, especially when they make you wait. Alone. The room has cameras and microphones, though they all appeared to be off. Kelli was not dumb enough to call someone and spill the beans on herself. She may not practice criminal law but she was still a very intelligent lawyer and knew how to keep from incriminating herself and she kept her trail clean. Or at least she hoped she had. She was about to find out. Just then in walked Governor Capp with two of her legal counsel.

"Hello Kelli, sorry about the wait." Capp said with an indifferent tone.

"Good afternoon Governor, and ladies." Kelli replied. Thinking to herself so much for the good old boy's club. All women in this meeting. No use trying to be pleasant. These bitches all had a reputation for cut throat tactics to get what they want.

"So, do you know why I asked you here today?" Capp asked.

"I'm not privy to your calendar Governor." Kelli replied sharply. As a consultant and not one of her official legal counsel, Kelli did not have the knowledge or authority that the other lawyers did.

"No you do not. And yet you seem to be interested in my where abouts. Why would that be?" Capp drilled back.

"Why don't you stop playing first year law school games and get on with it!" Kelli fired back.

"I could have you arrested and disbarred so you had better tone it down." Capp warned.

"Government intimidation is what is against the law here Governor, so you had better tone it down yourself." Kelli warned back. This was followed by silence. The tension in the room was on each of their faces. One of Capp's lawyers leaned over to her and said something near her ear. Kelli was ready to fight. She would not back down from anyone, and at this point felt she had nothing to lose. She obviously was going to need to look for another job.

" I want to remind you since you work for me you cannot help others with legal action against me." Capp declared.

"Wrong again Governor. I am a consultant only. And I'm sure your legal counsel knows that. So please do not try to overstep your bounds in giving legal advice or threats." Kelli replied.

Again Governor Capp's lawyer leaned over to whisper in her ear. Capp leaned back in her chair, obviously trying to come up with another strategy.

"Why are you so against me?" Capp asked.

"I never said I was. Why are we having this meeting?" Kelli shot back.

"That will be all. You can go." Capp announced.

"Go where? Back to work, or home?" Kelli asked.

"Back to work. For now." Capp said with a smile.

"Yes, ma'am." Kelli said back with a smile, and left

the room.

Kelli went back to her office. She kept an eye on the meeting room. They stayed in there for about an hour after she left. She thought Capp was going to fire her. She was sure Capp would have if her lawyers were not in the room. It is probably what she was warned against by her lawyer in the room when she whispered in the Governor's ear. So now what? Stick around or resign? She decided to sleep on it for a day or two. No need for a rush decision, at least not yet. But she did want to contact Jeff to find out what their side was up to. This may be the best time to switch sides.

33

The rays of light peaked in the window by their bed. Greg was laying on his left side with his arm around Marilyn, her back towards him. The early light, not much more than a night light in intensity, was casting over them from behind onto the far wall. He could barely see the old photos hanging on the wall. He knew what each was, for years he had stared at them in the morning light, wondering what it was like back then on the seas. No one in the photos was alive today, and even the boats were not around any longer. Lobstering back then was much more hands on, no electric winches to bring up the pots. They pulled pots in by hand from hundreds of feet under the water. The days were longer, and the longer one was on the water the more likely something was to go wrong. Nor'easters were extreme storms that could quickly come onto the Maine coast from the north eastern Atlantic, blowing mighty winds to the south west. When caught in a big one, it was unlikely anyone could make it home in one piece. Many a sailor died in such seas. The lucky ones limped into harbors up and down the coast taking on water and exhausted from fighting the sea. They had a story to tell, and all thanked the light that led them home.

How could he convey the importance of the lights to those in their past, to those who barely knew they were still there, and even worse, did not care if they were or not. Maybe it was time for the lights to go. No. No way. He could not give up. If only the lights were a

sports team of some kind. Die hard fans never seemed
to give up on their team, no matter how bad they were.
He thought other states, maybe countries, must be
having the same problem they were having. What if they
came together to start a Lighthouse League. Team
Maine, Team California, Team Michigan, Team Ohio,
etc. Friendly competition among them for best in many
classes of lighthouses. Spurring state pride, tourism
and trade, in sales of lighthouse memorabilia. And
education on lighthouses not only in the US, but world
wide. There are already many groups doing the work,
they just need to be brought together so they can help
one another. The more Greg imagined the possibilities
the more he got excited. He would start with a few
phone calls and take it from there.

He nudged Marilyn to wake her gently. He had to
tell her his idea. He was almost done before she woke
enough to understand the plan. She smiled at him, then
gave him a long kiss. She said, "Great idea but the sun
is not even up yet. It will be a great idea in an hour
also!"

"We need to get started calling around to see if there
is any interest. Then it may turn out to be a great idea!"
He exclaimed.

"If you call now you are just going to piss off a
bunch of people, especially those on the west coast, no
matter how great the idea is." She returned more awake
now. "Besides, I have an even better idea." As she
rolled towards him, ending up on top of him, then sitting
up over him, rocking ever so slowly. She pulled her top
off then she leaned forward for another kiss, slow and

sensuous. "This light house issue has been keeping us apart too much. We have to catch up on lost time."

He agreed, "I guess the lights can wait a bit longer. The west coast is three hours behind us, you're right, I would not want to piss anyone off." They slipped off the rest of their clothes. The sun was fully up by the time they both felt they had made up for lost time. They laid in bed again spooning each other. He said, "Thanks. I think your idea was better than mine."

She agreed this time, "Yes, but it's time to start calling the East coast teams. We have much work to do. So quit lollygagging and get up lazy head."

"Now it's my fault we are starting late." he said.

"Yep, always your fault. And I'm always right!" she exclaimed, as she jumped out of bed heading to the shower.

34

Governor Capp stormed into the conference room and slammed a notebook down on the table. Those in the room sat upright in their chairs, smiles gone, wondering what now! Yelling, "Why haven't any of you told me about those bastards trying to save those damn lighthouses. What are you doing here if you are not doing your job. All of you should have known, but none of you know what's going on. I get a call from a friend of mine telling me that the shit is about to hit the fan, making me look like a traitor to the state. Why the hell do I have to hear this shit from someone else? Does anyone in this damn room know about this?"

Silence. Thinking what the hell is she talking about. Looking at each other with a combination of question and fear on their faces. No one said a word.

Capp followed with, "That's exactly what I thought. You are all worthless to me. So get out, you're all fired!"

They just sat there. Was this real?

"I said get out! Security!" With that security came in, obviously on cue. And with a grand gesture, they all were walked out of the building. Actually fired from their public relation positions.

Her lawyers came in after the PR team left. Each took their usual places.

Capp began, "I hope all of you had time to look at the information I sent you. So let's put our heads together and come up with plan to stop them."

They talked for hours but Capp did not like what they were saying. She knew she could not fire all of them. But she had to do something. She was not going to just give up on the revenue she wanted, she needed, from the lights. It may not look good, but it is not actually illegal, so she decided to keep on with her plan, get the money and run. This was always her plan. She never planned on staying in Maine. This was just a means to an end. So she was gong all in. She knew there would be no way to turn back, no safety net. It would be all or nothing. Governor Capp told her legal team to prepare for the ride.

35

Marilyn and Greg spent the morning calling across the US, east to west, trying to garner support for the new Lighthouse League. There are twenty nine states with lighthouses. Some with only one, but not less important. The state with the most is not even on a coast, or at least not the east or west coast. It's on the north coast. Michigan, with over one hundred still active and at one time over two hundred. The next state in line is Maine. The exact number for each state is difficult to ascertain and depends on how they are counted. Anywhere from working lights in great condition to a pile of bricks with its only resemblance to a lighthouse in historical photos and a few peoples' memories of time gone by. Then there are faux lighthouses built in places for show rather than function. For example Nebraska has three. Most of these are private structures, but some are functioning lighthouses in the sense they have a light that could be used for navigational purposes. Some are on a body of water, lake or river, others not.

As they called around they did not discriminate location, just who wanted to help with the cause. Besides if Nebraska, Kansas and others wanted to use these lights for tourist attractions to help with state revenues then they were welcome to join the League. The main question the couple wanted to know, was there public access to the light and how much. How easy to get to the light, how close the public could get, and did they allow interior tours. Not many wanted to drive hundred of miles to find no access to see the lighthouse in any way.

The couple found great interest and support for their idea. Many asked why someone had not thought of this until now. Lighthouse enthusiasts face the same challenges across the US, even the world. They love an antiquated, outdated and eventually doomed structure. With a high cost of maintenance. It's hard to compare a static old structure to the ever moving and changing world. Just like still photography gave way to video. Greg called Jeff for legal advice on setting up a nonprofit to run the League. He was on board and assured Greg he would get things rolling and it should not take long. At this rate Greg felt they could go public with the League in about 2 weeks. Would that be quick enough to save Pemaquid from Capp's plan to sell it. He would not be surprised if she heard from someone what they were up to. There was no way to keep this a secret and get done quickly. He could only hope this would work. But maybe they would have to do a press release to prime the intrigue and interest in the League and in turn the lighthouses as a whole. He called Fred with an update and to set up a meeting in the next few days with the Pemaquid Lighthouse committee. That would give him a few days to get his pots checked and moved if needed.

36

This morning Marilyn and Greg were up before the sun. Marilyn agreed to help Greg with pots. They hoped to get them checked and set so to have a few days to work on the starting of the Lighthouse League. Marilyn was ahead of schedule on inspection of lights, so a day on the water with Greg was a welcome break. She felt comfortable now driving the boat, and because of that Greg was able to put more pots out. So far it was a great year for lobster numbers.

As they left the harbor she commented on the waves being a bit higher than in the past.

Greg responded, "We have a storm out in the Atlantic. It's quite a ways off shore and hopefully will stay there while moving north."

"And what if does not?" she asked.

"Then we are going to get wet!" he assured her.

She looked back at the shoreline vanishing behind her, and saw the beam from the Pemaquid light. Scared was not quite the right word, but definitely concerned, her stomach tightened into a small knot. She had witnessed the fury of waves crashing against the rocks by the lighthouse a few weeks ago during a storm. At the time they were almost beautiful. But now they were menacingly hitting the hull of the boat, with an occasional spray of cold water over the bow. More and more white caps were evident the further they went out into the darkening sea.

Greg announced, "We're here. Take the helm and follow the path."

The path was a series of dots on the screen in a serpentine pattern. Each dot represented a pot, and more specifically the buoy attached to the pot, moving about in the rough waters through which she was to maneuver the boat close enough so Greg could get a hook on the line. She had to take into account wind, waves, current, tide, and today a darkening sky. If she did not get close enough Greg would miss and she would have to loop around for another try, which wastes valuable time. This was especially true with the storm moving toward them more than northward as Greg had hoped.

Marilyn was piloting the boat like a professional captain. They were half way through the line of pots and Greg only missed one buoy due to her not getting close enough. She was able to loop around quickly to get back on the buoy for him to catch it. They were making good time and bringing in a good catch of lobsters. Greg emptied the pot they were on, then dropped it back in the water off the right side of the boat. It dove to the bottom quickly pulling the rope with it. Just as Greg threw in the buoy, a larger than usual wave hit the right side of the bow, pushing the boat counter clockwise in a circular pattern. The engine made a grinding sound and stopped suddenly. Marilyn did not know what happened, but Greg knew instantly. The back of the boat was spun into the heavy line between the pot and the buoy, wrapping it around the propeller. This was one of the worst things that could happen, even on a calm day. Often it required Greg to anchor then put on his wet suit and diving gear to unwrap or if bad enough, cut the rope away from the propeller and rudder losing the pot. There was no way he could go into the water with such a storm as they were in. He ran to the helm to try and get the boat running then assess how well he could steer.

Seeing the question of what happened on her face, "The pot rope got caught in the prop with the sudden spin from the wave. Cross your fingers we can get moving again."

The boat had been pushed a few hundred yards already without the engine running. Marilyn had been having to run the engine more than usual to keep in place against the constant push of the elements. So when the engine stopped it was almost like letting go of something attached to a stretched rubber band. If the pot was still attached it was being pulled along with them, it certainly was not heavy enough to anchor the boat in any way. Greg tried the engine a few time before it turned over. He did not have full power or full steering. So the rope was still attached. He would try to limp back into the harbor before being pushed onto the rocky shore. He could barely fight off the surge of the storm but was able to make up small ground to keep them from being pushed any longer. However he did not think he could make it all the way to the harbor so he had to come up with a Plan B.

Greg asked Marilyn, "Do you remember that old light on the small island near here?"

"Yes. It is still standing but not functioning. I don't

think we will be able to see it in this weather without a light." She answered.

"Agree. But it had a cove on the back side with good pilings still to tie off to. I think that will be our best chance right now." he suggested.

"You mean we are going to be ship wrecked out here!" she exclaimed.

"Well, hopefully not wrecked. Just a place to get out of the storm. Like a camping trip, sorta." He said with a smile.

"Are you crazy. That's not funny. You camp on solid ground, not on rolling waves!" she demanded.

Greg explained, "Take a deep breath. Good. Now here is the situation. I can tell by the way the engine is running and the steering that the rope is still there and affecting us. So we could take a chance getting back to harbor but when we get near the inlet we will need more power to keep off the rocks. I don't think we have enough power to do so. So, our best bet is to wait until after the storm to fix the problem, or motor in as is. We just need to get to the island dock and into the lighthouse to wait out the storm. It should be gone by morning."

Marilyn was a bit more calm after his plan, "It sounds like you've done this before?"

"Yes. This is just part of the job. Do whatever it takes to stay alive. We will be just fine." he assured her.

They followed the GPS map on the screen to the leeward side of the island, and were able to get into the cove. They tied off to the pilings. The dock was in disrepair but they cautiously navigated around the broken boards to make it to land. Greg carried his emergency pack he kept on the boat with supplies for just this occasion. He had taken refuge like this at least five times over the years. That was likely why he had never sunk his boat ending up in the water. He tried to learn from those before him. Not that he was a better captain, he just did not want to make the same misjudgment that others had that ended up with lost boats and lives.

The climb up the slippery path over wet rocks and moss made Marilyn question why lighthouses had to be on the highest spot in any area. Though she knew the actual answer, she just did not like this particular climb. The light was old and covered with vines and moss, but still quite sturdy made of heavy stones. The door was askew, partially hanging on rusty hinges. The cupola on top of the light was broken badly due to both rotting wood and heavy winds over the years. As they entered a bird flew out over their heads scaring Marilyn, she grabbed Greg. He just chuckled and kept going in with flashlight in hand. The hole in the cupola allowed a little rain in but more importantly made for a good draft from the door out the top. This allowed them to build a fire with some of the wooden crates and boards left inside decades ago. His water proof pack had fire starter materials, blankets, food and water. There was more than enough for the overnight stay they had in store. Once they arranged things around the fire it was quite comfortable and the storm seemed much less menacing inside the conical fortress.

"So, what do you think?" Greg asked.

"I guess this will do. I surely would rather be here than on the boat still, or in the water!" she pointed out.

"Are you hungry? I have survival food, how about some nuts. Good calorie input for the night. No wine, but water." he offered.

"Sure. So do you have to do this often?" she asked.

"Luckily no. Just when I want to be alone with a beautiful woman." he said with a smile.

"Doing it like this is against the law most places, it's called kidnapping when you plan it." she stated.

"No complaints so far." he responded.

"You wish you were that suave." She quipped.

"You are here. Warm romantic fire. Fine dining. View of the night sky. What more would any woman want? Would you want to be anywhere else?" he asked.

She hesitated then answered, "Not really I guess. Unless you were somewhere else, then you bet."

"Like floating in the ocean with waves crashing over our heads?" he asked.

"OK. You saved the day. Maybe you do have a little suave in you after all. By the way…" she looked down, "I'm sorry about causing all this."

"No. Do not do that. This is no one's fault. I could blame myself for even leaving the harbor in this weather. And even if it was we can not look back. The best way to survive is to continue looking forward. Asking what is, and looking for, the next best step." he lectured sternly.

"Yes sir. You sound like my old English teacher drilling us on proper grammar. So what is the next step?" she asked.

"What do you think?" he asked back.

She thought for a moment, looked up into his eyes and gave him a long kiss.

"I was going to say, keep the fire going, keep hydrated, fix the boat in the morning and head back to the harbor. But I do like your plan better." Greg said softly. "And though I was planning on Pemaquid, this is a lighthouse still, and the one that is saving us tonight, so I can not wait. Or want to lose this thing." Greg reached into his pants pocket retrieving a small pouch. As he opened the pouch retrieving its contents, "Marilyn, I love you more than I ever knew imaginable, even more than checking pots." He said with a smile, and continued, "So, Marilyn will you marry me?" He held up the ring. She recognized it, or thought she did, her father used to let her hold her mother's ring when she was young to help remember her by. She said yes, and then asked where he got the ring.

As he placed it on her finger he said, "It was your mother's, and her mother's before. Your father gave it to me when I asked him for your hand."

Marilyn was stunned, she could not take her eyes off the ring, memories flooded her mind and heart. Tears flowed down her cheeks. She finally whispered, "It's perfect, beautiful and could not have been more of a surprise. I love you so much."

They kissed more, cried happy tears together affirming their love, then snuggled in the blankets helping keep each other warm.

37

Marilyn and Greg returned to the harbor the next morning without incident. Greg dove under the boat when back to find no rope or problem with the prop or rudder. The way the boat ran that morning he felt the rope must have come off overnight while bobbing around in the storm. They took care of their catch and prepped the boat for the next run. Greg's phone buzzed. After reading the text he told Marilyn there was an emergency meeting of the new Lighthouse League organizers at noon. They would have time to go home and get cleaned up as well as get something to eat before going. As they drove home Marilyn looked at all the scenery from the harbor to Pemaquid Light and for the first time really felt like she was a part of this life. She was not just here for a job. This was her home now. All of this. She reached over and held Greg's hand somewhere along the way, the bright after storm sunlight sparkled off her ring. He pulled up to the lighthouse and shut off the truck, they both sat their looking at Pemaquid Light. It seemed like forever since they left just yesterday morning. Just a day in the life of a Maine lobsterman.

Marilyn asked, "So, when do we go back out to check the rest of the pots?"

Greg gave her one of his smiles, "I think you're hooked, Mrs. Smith. We'll shoot for tomorrow, depending on what goes on at this meeting."

Marilyn responded, "I like the sound of that Mr.

Smith. As for the meeting, a nap sounds more appealing at the moment. But we need to save this light. I'm ready to fight, do whatever it takes to stop Governor Capp."

Greg agreed as they went inside to get ready for the meeting.

38

Greg had radioed the Harbor yesterday that they were seeking shelter on the island to wait out the storm. He did not want the rescue team to send out boats and planes to try and find him. So everyone had heard of their ordeal when they showed up for the meeting, but not the real news. As expected there were many inquiries about their health and the boat's condition. As well as support and acceptance of Marilyn as Greg's bride to be, as if the ordeal was her initiation into their club. Both made Marilyn feel more like one of the group now. And she liked that very much.

Fred called the meeting to order, "Let's all get seated so we can get started. Thank you all for coming. I am sure all of you are as surprised and delighted with the turn of events over the past day. It looks like this will all be behind us soon. And not only will we be able to keep our lights but with the new Lighthouse League we shall ensure their safety from others with like minded intent to sell off these national treasures."

Greg and Marilyn looked at each other puzzled. What was he talking about? Greg raised his hand, "Sorry for interrupting, but what is gong on? I think Marilyn and I missed something."

A regular piped up, "Maybe a little less island romance and more keeping your eye on your lines, you'd of made it back yesterday. Or Gregory was it all in your plans from the start?" He finished with a snort and a laugh, since all were OK now.

The others laughed a bit as well.

Marilyn replied quickly, "No. It really was…" then she stopped realizing they were just doing what they do. She laughed too and admitted, "You're right you caught us. But actually it was my idea!"

Now they all really laughed.

"Go get him girl." Someone said from the back.

Danielle spoke up, "Sorry girls, but she got him alright. He's a goner. Time to find someone else to be our most valuable bachelor."

With that Marilyn leaned over and gave Greg a big kiss as if marking her territory.

Fred intervened, "Enough of the foolishness now. Though we are very glad to have you Marilyn. I guess we did not think to make sure you knew. Governor Capp has resigned. Seems once the sale of the lights came to light investigators found more than anyone expected of her back room dealings. And they still are uncovering more. I am going to let Jeff give everyone the details."

Jeff came to the front of the room, "Thank you Fred. And I agree with Fred, Marilyn we all are very glad to have you as officially one of us now." A big applause erupted. "It has really been a team effort. And Greg's epiphany in the formation of the Lighthouse League was the actual event that made all this happen. The support garnered from around the country, and now the world, since this went viral on social media was nothing short of a miracle. We have other countries wanting to join the League. And most of all, as of an hour ago, over one hundred million fans world wide are ready to join our cause." Another big applause broke out followed by the chant Team Maine, Team Maine, Team Main… "Yes, that's right. It is true hysteria among the fans. And because of that I have brought on another attorney to help start the League. Kelli Masters was another invaluable patriot of our cause and we are not only glad but privileged to have her formally on our team. Kelli please stand up so everyone can see who you are. Most of you do not know her but please give her a welcoming thank you." Applause all around again. "And feel free to extend your personal gratitude to her after the meeting. More details on exactly what all irregularities and illegalities were going on at the State House will be coming out over the next few days and weeks I'm sure. But for now, the acting Governor has assured us that any sale of the lights or the property around them has halted and will no longer be entertained."

39

Marilyn and Gregory pulled up to their home next to the majestic Pemaquid Light standing tall in the bright sunshine with the sound of waves gently breaking on the rocks beneath her and birds flying over her. It had been a great two weeks traveling along the East Coast inspecting lights. As much fun as they both had had, there was no light like their own. It was always special retuning from a work trip for them.

She gently touched his arm saying, "Honey we're home. Time to wake up sleepy head."

He woke slowly, the bright sunlight making him squint as he got out of the vehicle. Then he recognized someone and took off running into John's arms, yelling, "Grandpa!"

John gave him a big hug, picking him up in his arms.

Greg came out to meet them, giving Marilyn a hug and a kiss. Then asked Gregory, "Hey buddy, did you learn anything this trip?"

He replied, "You bet. I'll tell you all about it while we check pots. You waited for me didn't you?"

Greg said, "As always. You know you're my good luck mate."

Marilyn chimed in, "What about me? Am I invited?"

Gregory asked, "Dad we could use a pilot, what do you think?"

Greg affirmed, "Yep, it sure would make things easier. That is if you're up to it after your drive."

Marilyn snapped, "It's never stopped me in the past. One of my favorite things to do. But I have to check on brother and sister."

With that Shari said as she came out of the house, "The twins just fell asleep for their nap. We have them, go ahead, they will be waiting for you when you get back."

Marilyn gave Greg a kiss, saying, "Life just keeps getting better."